Run Baby Run

by

Michael Allen Zell

Lavender Ink
New Orleans
lavenderink.org

Run Baby Run
by Michael Allen Zell
Copyright © 2015 by Michael Allen Zell and Lavender Ink
All rites reserved. No part of this work may be reproduced etc.

Printed in the U.S.A.
First Printing
10 9 8 7 6 5 4 3 2 1   15 16 17 18 19 20

Cover and Book design: Bill Lavender

Library of Congress Control Number: 2015935098
Zell, Michael.
Run Baby Run / Michael Allen Zell
p. cm.

ISBN: 978-1-935084-84-6 (pbk.)

Run Baby Run

Tell me what we gonna do
If everything I say is true

—Curtis Mayfield

For Rebecca

1

Toes finished his walk up St. Ferdinand. He was at his destination. Sweat was dripping down his back and from his underarms.

"I've been waking up all day long," he said.

He stood almost six foot tall but walked like a shorter man. Skin the color of glue. It glowed in the moonlight. He sported an ironic moustache that had grown in stride with his acclaim. It fluttered in the light breeze. His face was that of a young man who hadn't seen many rough days, though he was thirty-six. His long black t-shirt featured the logo of a skateboard company. Tan cargo shorts peeked out underneath. Shoes far too expensive for the rest of the get-up completed him.

It was early June, only a month into summer. Elsewhere, people slept. They cooked up tidy elixirs in the dreamland mind. Some of those people lived in New Orleans, but their number was limited. The Other City was in full swing and only midway through the night. Didn't matter that it was 4:00 a.m. on Sunday. Same thing would be happening any night. No need for last call at the bars. Some of them didn't have locks for the doors since they never closed. The bars paid the bills, kept the above-ground economy humming.

Much of the Other City bolstered the underground economy too. Who didn't need to scratch an itch? Third trick wasn't just the name for a workman's shift. No, this time of night the city opened her sweaty arms and said, "Bring me your huddled masses, and I'll leave them staggering in the streets and trembling between the legs of strangers by daybreak. For a cost."

Toes opened his backpack. Though he was conscious of what surrounded him, he'd waited in this spot a few minutes to make sure no one came out from the shadows. He had his buzz on. Whiskey. Enough to get in the zone.

That was part of his ritual. So too that the cans of Ironlak spray paint he took out were stolen. Also, that he spoke softly to himself, becoming at ease with his canvas.

"I've been waking up all day long," he said again.

It sounded like a good line. He added to it. "I've been waking up all day long. That's the only way to live in a song." Toes repeated the lines with his whiskey lips while he took out the special nozzles used for certain types of lines. He shook his head thinking about Rusto and Krylon changing their valves to discourage their products' usage by graffiti writers.

"It's a perfect place," he said, scanning the area more directly. Toes stood alongside the concrete columns at the riverside of North Robertson and St. Ferdinand. The posts supported the elevated portion of the road that bridged over the train yard.

"Yes, it's perfect. I can't believe these haven't been touched." Traffic couldn't see him. Only one light working up above. He was otherwise almost surrounded by dead end streets. Train tracks to his right. Only a few were brought by residence or intention. You didn't end up there otherwise unless you made a series of wrong turns.

"I'll just need to keep checking," he said, watching back to where the street led to St. Claude.

As Toes turned around to the columns, he looked at the moon and at the five story building shadowing the tracks on the other side of the overpass. It was why he was there.

"I've been waking up all day long, but you can't have my song," he sang.

For decades it was Schneider Paper Products. Sign still on the upper part of the building. Schneider moved to Baton

Rouge after the flood Hurricane Katrina triggered and the levees released.

Toes was on a roll. He started with the first column while he continued speaking. His name came from the Toehead figures he'd concocted. Humans, animals, aliens. All with toes for the top of their heads. First, the outline in black.

"The paper people move away and you out-of-towners take over and call it the Papier Art Gallery," Toes muttered, conveniently forgetting he'd come to New Orleans just a few years before from New York as a college student.

"It's like the suburbs. Name something after what's no longer there. Complete opposite of war time. The victorious would never name a place after the defeated," he continued as the bird figure began to take shape.

"Away from war, guilt and nostalgia count most. Chop down acres of apple orchard and call it Apple Orchard Estates," he said, remembering the subdivision where he'd grown up.

"You start an art gallery and put out word you want *me* to do Toeheads inside your place, on your walls," he fired and grabbed another paint can to add color.

"No way. You can't have my song," He attached the nozzle for shading.

Toes had heard that the gallery owners, Brendan and Juniper, in actuality both originally upstate New Yorkers like himself, had seen his work on the columns where Almonaster met Alvar, near the Danziger Bridge that crossed the Industrial Canal. That was his signature move. Toeheads on cylindrical surfaces.

"You can't have me. Fuck off," he said, feeling the effects of the whiskey and using a dark blue to double a few lines. His own deals with developers to use graffiti as a selling tool for their condos couldn't have been further from his mind.

Toes had come a long way. His given name was Tyler Dolan.

Tyler had gone to school to follow in his father's footsteps as a business litigation attorney. In the aftermath of the 2005 disaster, he started collecting abandoned wood and the contents of houses put to the sidewalks and streets. Made art from the muck and disregard. In spite of never having done it before, his pieces were a hit. Family money helped, once Tyler was able to convince his father of a hefty return on his investment.

"I like how this is coming along," Toes said. He rummaged through his backpack for an accent mark nozzle.

Few in his known world as Tyler had any idea that he also did graffiti writing. Though he was the owner of a nice Marigny double shotgun house, in which he occupied both sides, Tyler craved his world as Toes. Skateboarding around rough neighborhoods. Graffiti writing. It was like the New York he wasn't allowed to have growing up.

Toes checked his back, then around. No one here. Just the random car zipping by twenty feet above him. He checked his watch.

"Good, good. Took fifteen minutes to do this one," he said. "Time to sign it."

Toes turned sideways to spray the letters that ran vertically alongside the Toehead so that the bottoms of the large "T" and smaller "oes" faced the bird from the side. He stepped back to take it all in.

As he did, there was movement at his immediate right from the rubble piled up alongside the other concrete columns.

Toes stepped forward and quickly pulled pepper spray from his backpack before tossing the paint cans and nozzles inside. He zipped up the backpack and flung it over his shoulders, all while intently watching the moving rubble. "The fuck you want?" he said in a voice with a lump in it.

The rubble turned into a shadow that continued toward him.

Toes spoke up louder, betraying his private school education with feigned toughness. "I said, 'What the fuck do you want?'" His face tightened. Each end of his moustache coiled as if ready to strike.

The shadow took one more step, now moving into the faint glow of the body shop security light directly on the other side of the overpass. He was a black man in his 40's who looked older. Wore a dirty button-up short sleeve shirt and dirtier blue jeans. His shoes were ribbons and his aroma was piss.

"The fuck *I* want? Me?" he said. "Shiiiit. S'all about what *you* want."

Toes tried to make himself strong. The legend and ritual of infamous Toes, at least in his own mind, was quickly sinking. He had become Tyler Dolan again and was out of his element.

"I'm living in a song. It's my song," he said to himself.

The man spoke again. "Bernell got what you want. You want weed? Some dogfood? What you want?"

Toes was barely holding onto himself. His moustache ends twitched as if attempting to bore themselves into his cheeks to hide. "I don't need any pot. Definitely not…dogfood."

Bernell took another step forward, the lines in his face and the glint in his eyes becoming more prominent. "C'mon, man. Alla them artists and most ev'rybody shootin' dogfood now."

He looked at Toes holding up the pepper spray like a crossing guard adamant at protecting children in the intersection from cars. Bernell shook his head. "Shiiiit." He sighed and put on his whitefolks voice, all enunciation and intact syllables. "Sir… do you want to buy some heroin? It's good for your artistic expression."

Toes replied, "No, no, no. I just use a little molly and pot, but I don't need anything."

While speaking, Bernell slipped his right hand into his back pocket. He looked to his left at the train tracks to guide Toes' eyes while the shaky hand came out full.

Bernell took one more step. His uncombed hair rose in tufts and further confirmed as homeless or close to it. He was thinking, "Simple son of a bitch. Too easy to okey doke him."

Toes moved in kind, backward to Bernell's forward motion. Toes had no more songs in his soul.

Bernell began to run forward with the motion of a man barely out of a nap. He stepped into a crater-sized pothole unlit by the moon, the body shop security light, or the one working lamp post out of fourteen along the river side of the overpass. Went in up to his shins and fell forward, banging up his knees. His paring knife sprung from his hand and skipped along the street, right to Toes.

It happened so quickly that they both were wordless, the new potholed supplicant and the other in a surprising position of power.

Toes bent down and picked up the knife with his left hand while assuring, "I'm not going to use it. Don't worry."

Bernell was over his shock at being disarmed and now felt only disgust. "Get it over with. Man come at you, gonna stick you, you gotta get him. Do it. Get it over with. Stick me."

Toes put the pepper spray in his front shorts pocket and pulled out a wad of bills.

He put the money in his left hand with the knife, walked to the crater, and pulled the astonished Bernell up with his right hand.

"You just need money for food, right?" Toes asked.

Bernell looked at him quizzically, an odd bleach-white man offering a knife and money.

"This a trick?"

"Oh, no. No, sir. Here, take this."

Toes handed the knife and $87 to Bernell.

"This mine? You playin' me?"

"You need it more than I do."

Bernell, still expecting a trick, tentatively took it all from Toes. "Alright," he said.

Toes smiled, now secure in his patronizing position.

Bernell turned and hobbled away from Toes, under the overpass, ending up back in the shadows.

Toes felt relief that no one had come to harm and he'd done a good deed. "I've been waking up all day long," he sang.

A couple cars barreled along the initial incline of the overpass far too quickly. He stepped back to look upward, only to see a jeep rise into the air and a man expelled from it.

In an instant, the flying man struck the guardrail and the jeep slammed against him. This all occurred in a matter of milliseconds. The sound of speed, the jumping jeep, and the pinned man screaming and staring at Toes with eyes of horror.

Before Toes could move, an object was rapidly flung from the action above. Hit him square in the face. "Uhhh," he moaned. His nose was broken, moustache curdled, and he landed flat on his back, knocked out.

In the twenty or so minutes Toes lay passed out, New Orleans was busy.

The first death of Sunday, June 8th, homicide by car, had of course already occurred almost simultaneously with the brief incapacitation of Toes.

Shortly after, a security guard driving home from work had his Honda Civic t-boned by a red light runner at nearby Franklin and Claiborne. This was the first auto collision involving two vehicles.

A new Infiniti was stolen from an apartment courtyard way out on Chef Menteur, just past the cluster of Vietnamese restaurants and shops. This registered it as the first of what would be six car thefts for the day, hitting the city's daily average firmly.

As with many of the others, the Infiniti was driven to a body shop, stripped expertly, and the tires were added to a pile that would be eventually sold off. Everything else was loaded up in a truck to sell at one of the numerous local salvage yards that paid cash for scrap metal. They were legally required to record seller information and issue a check, but that was routinely disregarded.

The firsts of the day also included fifteen young men and seven young women who lost their virginity, along with thirty-one tourists (three of the men also lost their wallets in the aftermath of their deflowering), and one foolish guy in his early 20's who only said he was a virgin online for what he thought would be an easy pick-up.

When he showed up at the only inhabited house in an otherwise weed-covered Lower 9th Ward block, he was met by more than the temptress seen on the dating site. Five men intended to steal his car and were so angry that he'd had the nerve to waste their time by biking all the way there that they beat him with his bike. Next they stripped him down and dumped him out of their car along the Claiborne Bridge, making for a particularly harrowing first simple battery of the day, with a kidnapping thrown in to boot.

A 24-hour market in St. Roch also had a first, their initial drop-off of goods for the coming week. Elastically named Cajun Creole Supermarket, though owned by a Gretna man from a wholly other part of the world, they got their food from one source and everything else from others. The batch of stolen smart phones arrived just in time to start the week, along with boxes of sandwich bags, roses in glass tubes, shoelaces, steel wool pads, and spoons. Variations of this drop-off occurred at nine other corner markets around New Orleans.

Among other events in New Orleans while Toes was flat on his back, two children were born.

In the other direction, along River Road in Kenner, a baker's dozen of late night marathon runners were pacing themselves back to Orleans Parish. One of them called out the time, "4:45," but of course Toes couldn't hear him.

Toes wobbled to his feet. Nose was dripping blood. He had black eyes and bruised cheeks. Moustache was mangled. The backpack that cushioned his fall didn't prevent a concussion.

With an odd sense of woozy purpose, Toes picked up the heavy cardboard Abita Amber beer case that sat undisturbed next to him. He began swaying down the street with confusion.

His speech had purpose before, but now he muttered and squinted.

"Rooster…green…ceiling fan," he sputtered. The gibberish made complete sense to him.

He swayed and stumbled along Rudy's Auto Repair on his right and the tall green warehouse across the street.

Toes continued through the Villere intersection, past a variety of little houses. Though he saw no one and was only bidden by his mission of carrying the case with both arms, a few eyes saw him, a milk-white man dripping red blood.

More eyes behind windows were alert by the time he made it at his slow pace to the next cross street. There had been a horrific crime a few months ago on the block of Urquhart to his right, and the neighbors were still uneasy.

A drug dealer had been getting high and playing video games with three others while a woman they called Bucketmouth pleasured each of them in turn. Three members of a competing gang broke in, held them all hostage, demanded the money, and killed two of them before the naked young woman led the assailants to the stash.

The upper body of Toes swung in a semi-circle with feet rooted to the ground as he paused, before internal radar led him off St. Ferdinand and on to his left. "Rooster…red…

ceiling fan," louder this time.

There was only one block of Urquhart left before the train tracks. Toes veered to the left side of the street.

Woozy radar led him along a series of fences. His left elbow bumped first against the chain link fence, rattling it. The rattle turned into a dull thud when the fence became wood, then metal. By the time the fence was cinderblock and he moved past it, his scuffed elbow began to bleed. The last part of the fence, merely scraps of tin and wood, before opening up to the train yard, delivered the final blow.

"Rooster...yellow...ceiling span," he said, louder than before, in further pain from the jagged metal and nails catching his now pulpy left elbow.

But yet, he held the beer case firmly. Bloody nose continued dripping, building up on his shirt and shorts, a few drops still making it to the street.

A gravel and pothole filled stretch was alongside the tracks. Toes stumbled through it all.

The railroad yard began to widen at Marais, a parallel block toward the river, and continued to swell with tracks until its widest point between Claiborne and Galvez.

New Orleans' initial existence came to be as a port city. The trains and yards were a reminder that despite modern changes, the city existed to ship goods in and out. Tracks threaded the city and surrounding areas, from St. Bernard to upriver, along I-610, through Old Metairie, alongside Airline Highway, and more.

Navigation of the tracks at hand by Toes was a different matter. His broken nose and jumbled mind led him forward.

Initially he bumped his feet on the train tracks and stopped. In his confusion, he was trudging through a few feet of flood water, saving paper products.

"Rooster...ripple...ceiling span," he told the world while

he lifted his legs high through the imaginary water. Box held above his head to keep it dry for the crossing.

High-stepping like he was crossing a swollen creek, Toes maneuvered through the series of metal tracks, wooden ties, and gravel filler. He bobbed and weaved, asserted and complied. Had any eyes been on him, they'd not have expected him to make it across but instead pitch forward on his face.

Toes looked to his right, where the tracks led to the river. He leaned back to tilt his head up at the moon a little to the left of the Crescent City Connection bridge.

In doing so, along with the weight of the beer case above his head, gravity almost got the better of him and sent him down again on his back.

He groaned and swayed, righting himself and high-stepping like a Clydesdale horse over the last couple sets of tracks.

At least he could walk normally again, which still resembled a drunkard's shamble or zombie shuffle. He was also able to drop the beer case to his chest. Trouble averted. Imaginary paper products kept dry.

On the downriver side of the train yard, a chain link fence might've been an obstacle to his forward drive but for the fact that it had been crudely torn open as if by a train itself.

Toes moved through it, pleased in some way, despite his state.

"Rooster…red…all day long," he hollered.

The mission of Toes continued along Urquhart, past the long linen services building on the right that spanned the block.

A few doors across Feliciana, he paused and registered in a distorted-mind way the music lightly heard over the wooden fence to his right. He loudly added a variation to his refrain, which in turn could be heard by those inside the fence. At first there were chuckles of bewilderment at how the clumsy braying matched up to the song playing.

"Nina Simone's not a rooster! No pizza for you," a husky voice called out.

The response struck Toes as a threat, reeling as he was.

He lurched to the other side of the street, bumping into a parked food truck that had Bentley's Meals on Wheels painted along the side.

This continuing threat compelled him to take the next left, turning on Clouet. Toes kept to the middle of the street.

He steadied himself midway before Villere on a For Sale sign posted between the street and the sidewalk. He was out of breath and drenched with sweat. Both his nose and elbow had stopped bleeding, though the former was bent to the side and the latter was a raw mess.

Soft voices carried through the summer air. "Can you believe…" "I know, right."

Toes turned and saw them coming from the direction he'd slowly taken. Two young women on bicycles. Both variations on the other. Summer dresses, clunky boots, flowery head pieces, devil-may-care attitudes.

Feeling threatened again, Toes put down the case and pulled out a can of spray paint from his backpack. It was then they saw him and slowed.

"Are you okay?" "He seems dazed."

Toes came to life, stomping heavily toward them and spraying each with dark blue paint.

"Nina Simone…not…my…song," he yelled at them.

They biked off, cursing. Toes was now facing the boarded-up former Lorraine Hansberry Elementary School, its periphery surrounded by ten foot tall chain link, which was topped with barbed wire. In the recesses of his bruised mind, coherence wanted to return, triggered by the abandoned building untouched by spray paint. He grunted, but it didn't become a known thought.

He dropped the can on the street, retrieved the cardboard beer case, and proceeded up to Robertson, which was now at street level. Due to the confrontation delaying his journey, a tow truck pulling a white SUV sped past seconds before he entered the roadway.

Led by the unknown, Toes continued on Clouet, beyond the church van parked on the right that would be picking up congregants for service at New Life Baptist Church in a few hours. He kept on. Across Claiborne, which was typically busy. Past the blighted house on the left with a sign indicating it was soon to be demolished. Past Derbigny. He came to a little alley on the right.

He grinned with a simple-minded mouth.

His mind didn't register then or ever that his eyes next saw the sign reading Industrial Court, didn't know that he followed it, nor that he collapsed alongside the house at the end, beer box by his side.

2

Hutch yanked the steering wheel to pull the bucking jeep out of the guard rail. It all happened so quickly, whatever was in the road that he hit, launching the jeep skyward. Clint was catapulted out of it and jammed up against the guard rail. From Clint's screams, Hutch had a bad feeling his partner had just been sandwiched and smashed to death.

"Damn," he thought, "Should've got a fuckin' canvas top for the jeep."

None of the plan was going accordingly. The big white SUV was still chasing him, his getaway was going the wrong direction, and he had no partner anymore. Was the money still safe on the floor where Clint's feet had been? He was driving too fast to look down.

Hutch didn't know this area. He'd grown up in Gert Town, stayed in Marrero across the river for years, and worked in the French Quarter.

As he sped on Robertson, elevated across the train yard, he caught a glimpse in his peripheral vision. It gave him an idea, but he'd have to act quickly. The SUV was barreling forward in the left lane.

"Double back, double back," he repeated like a mantra.

This needed to work perfectly, otherwise they'd keep on following him like they had from the Quarter.

To trick them, he sped up and passed the next three blocks with the speedometer needle pushing above 75 mph. Robertson was back down to street level.

The SUV increased speed as well and pulled up alongside him. Hutch could sense they were edging over and trying to match his speed perfectly. He took a gamble they were about to ram the jeep off the road.

Between Clouet and Louisa, a long brick cemetery wall ran the entire length along the right-hand side.

Hutch thought, "Alright, just past this. Then I get up outta here."

He let off the gas and lightly tapped the brakes before reaching the next corner. Not enough to jolt him forward, but a deceleration of at least 20 mph.

As he did this, the SUV pulled hard and fast to the right, intending to strike metal with metal. Instead it met air, which yielded quicker than expected.

In a perfect crisscross, Hutch was able to turn from the right lane and make a left on Piety. He heard the boom behind him. The SUV drove into the house on the downriver corner of the street.

It was an odd structure, a four room long shotgun double used as a single. The front door originally on the right side for that unit had been filled and covered with weatherboards. This made the structure look off-kilter, what with only a left side front door and no windows. The steps to the porch running right down the middle had a rail on only the right side, further confusing the eye.

Those were the structural idiosyncrasies before the roaring Ford Explorer entered the house.

Luckily for the next door neighbor, the SUV didn't also make it into his place. The vehicle plowed through the front parlor of the corner shotgun from the side. The still-existing front middle wall and fireplace slowed it enough so that only the front of the vehicle made it through the opposite outside wall.

The two adult women sleeping in the middle rooms immediately awoke and flung themselves to the floor, grabbing the three little ones with them. They thought it was gunshots or a bomb, not expecting an SUV had demolished part of the house.

The two men inside the vehicle looked at each other, cursed, locked their doors, and pulled out all of their guns. They put a couple of them on the dashboard and held the others tightly. The driver Johnny grimaced and sighed.

"Boss is gonna be fucking mad," he said while taking out his phone and dialing.

Simultaneous to all of this, Hutch took Piety up a block to Claiborne, doubling back the same direction he'd come from. Like Robertson, Claiborne was elevated above the train yard.

"Guess I'm gonna have to do all this shit myself," Hutch said.

Then it hit him.

"But I keep all the money. If it didn't fly out the jeep."

In his exuberance to check on the money and with the recent experience of running several stoplights in the chase, Hutch ran the red light at Claiborne and Franklin. He'd slowed his speed but totaled the jeep and a little Honda Civic he struck. Both mangled front ends.

The other driver was a slight young man on his way home from a security job that paid minimum wage. The Civic was how he kept from relying on infrequent buses that would make his shift across town run more than an extra hour. He got out of his car pushed near the neutral ground and crumpled by the jeep still up in it.

"What the fuck!" he said, shoulders pulled back for conflict.

Hutch stepped out of the jeep with a different look. He wasn't mad. He was full-on furious. He'd just realized that the beer case flew out of the jeep with Clint, so he had no money, no partner, no car, and rough characters were looking for him. He limped over to the security guard, his left knee banged up in the crash.

Holding his hands up in an appearance of appeasement, he said, "Sorry, little brother."

With a quick left, Hutch rabbit punched the man and followed it up with a powerful right. Put him down so fast the security guard fell right into nap time.

Hutch limped over to the sidewalk, leaving the smaller man prone on the ground behind him.

"Don't know what I'm gonna do, but I got to get off the street," he said.

There were no witnesses to his hobbling along Franklin. Had there been, they'd have seen a man in his early 50's. He was solidly built, with a face and complexion similar enough to that of Motown star Willie Hutch from decades back.

Hutch, whose legal name was Raymond Pate, liked the high school nickname, especially since everyone had called his best friend "Raymond at the end of the block" to differentiate them. Hutch was better. Tight. Tough. A good name during his boxing days.

He was now twenty years past his prime but still strong enough to handle the out-of-control drunks and belligerent types as a bouncer at Club Big Easy in the 500 block of Bourbon. Hadn't forgotten how to knock a man out with a punch, like the guy on the ground.

New Orleans and the West Bank were home. Pops had a heart attack after seeing his drowned house after the flood, but Hutch couldn't imagine keeping a few hustles going anywhere else. Moms wasn't on this earth either. Who knew where his brother Eric had gone?

Hutch was dressed in black from head to toe, same as he'd been at work. He wouldn't be able to blend into the night much longer, though. Daylight would be coming.

Wincing from his tender knee, he tried to walk on the side of his foot, wincing harder at the idea he now had no home.

Couldn't stay in New Orleans. No new place to go to either, what with the money gone.

Hutch couldn't have felt more helpless, more alone, but for a moment he also considered himself blessed.

Two doors before the next Franklin intersection stood an abandoned building. The little house just past it was tidy. Flowers in front, flag holder, the whole deal. This other building, though, was a mess.

The façade was tan-colored stucco with three large grey paint blotches partly covered by larger brown ones to mask the graffiti already coming back. There were three second floor windows with metal canopies.

Hutch nodded in approval. This would work as a hide-out for now, but how to get in?

Both iron doors were locked. The one in the middle with a garage door next to it, also locked, must've been for the business. The door on the left had steps behind it and was a ½ address. Former upstairs apartment.

Hutch was now determined. "This is good," he said softly. A difficult place to get into probably meant no other inhabitants, and he could stay there as long as needed.

There were chain link gates on both sides of the building. The one on the left was used by the tidy-house-occupants to protect their car and a swing. The one on the right had nothing behind it but overgrown weeds. Easy choice.

Hutch scaled the gate. It normally would've been a simple move, but with his banged-up knee, he went over sideways, like a track high jumper extending over a pole with legs as scissors. "Motherfuckin'sonofafuckin'bitch," he said, due to the strain.

Hutch ran his hands over his sweaty forehead.

After climbing over a second chain link gate in the rear, he shouldered open the rotted back door.

"This building ain't been occupied since Katrina. Maybe

longer than that," he said.

He limped up the stairs, feeling the mold already getting into his system.

"Aw, hell no," Hutch said, remembering how the black mold had irritated his nose and mouth when gutting a few houses. Eventually he had to stop doing favors, because his body couldn't handle it.

The second floor was a mix of detritus and disarray. The roof was open to the sky in spots, so the mildew and mold was fresh and strong from occasional rain. Anything of potential value had been taken away for reuse or cash. All that was left was in the process of disintegration. The stench was overwhelming.

Hutch's eyes stung, but only from the mold. He was in a shitload of trouble. His world was rapidly getting smaller. A target was on his back. But he was a tough character himself.

"Be strong, Hutch. Keep it together. Done some dirt in my life, but this is a whole lotta mess," he said.

He hobbled over to the closest window overlooking the street, being careful not to walk under the roof holes. Hutch assumed that years of rain had rotted the floorboards. Termites, attracted by the moisture, likely would've turned the wood to sponge.

Hutch looked out at Franklin and the closed Chinese restaurant across the street. He was immediately reminded of how the whole thing came about. Stretching out on the floor next to the window, the conversation with Clint at the Chinese place in the Quarter about a month ago bombarded his mind.

"What's the deal? Shit, Clint, couldn't we talk about this at work?"

"Hutch, Hutch, take it easy. Tell me the chicken isn't all that."

"Yeah, it's good, but why we here on Dauphine? Not for the food. C'mon, man. Placate me."

"Okay, okay. Here it is. I heard crazy stuff at the club yesterday. Been thinkin' about it. I got in early. Had to bring my bitters and tinctures I made at home."

"Nobody buys those science drinks. They want the cheapest thing get them drunk off their ass."

"I'm a mixologist, Hutch. It's an art. Mr. C gave me the bar on the 2nd floor for a reason. Upscale crowd."

"Alright, alright. So you get in early."

"And I'm upstairs, crouched below the bar, puttin' my bag away and organizing. Mr. C comes in on the phone. I'm about to stand up, but I hear what he's saying. The boss was givin' him the new safe combination and made Mr. C repeat it back to him. Turns out they change it every few months."

"C'mon. Don't talk stupid."

"No, wait. Listen to this. Got your game face on, Hutch?"

"Please. You got nothin' more I wanna know."

"Hutch, you definitely wanna hear this. Our safe – the safe at Club Big Easy – is where they keep the skims from all four of the clubs the boss owns on Bourbon. It's a mix of video poker and skims from the house. Plus all the other…"

"C'mon. I…"

"Hutch, they keep almost…"

"Nah, I'm good. Stop playin'."

"…a million dollars in that safe."

"Whoa. You serious? On the real?"

"Yeah. You see my face. I'm not playin'. I'd heard they trade all the cash out at the bank for new $100 bills before it goes to the boss."

"Why you tellin' me? You want the black man to take the fall, huh?"

"I'm tellin' you 'cause this is a two-man job, and you definitely want the action."

"How you see that?"

"That's the best part. Every Sunday at 3:30 a.m., Mr C sends his two guys out for the money, then goes downstairs, picks out someone, and takes him out back to that room in the courtyard."

"I seen it. I don't like that shit, but I know what he does."

"That means nobody's in the office, Hutch. Nobody's watching the cameras."

"And all that paper just sittin' there for you, huh?"

"Yeah. For *us*. You gotta take care of things on the 1st floor. Make sure Mr. C doesn't come back upstairs. Make sure Johnny and Big T don't come up if they get back early."

"We do this, we dead men."

"Not if we leave New Orleans immediately. We disappear. It's all skims, so they can't go to the feds."

"I'm not worried 'bout no feds. Any of them – Mr. C, Johnny, Big T – boss have any of them put a bullet in my black head and your white one."

"But what if you could get away, could go away?"

"Sure, I seen a few countries on the Travel Channel. But, c'mon, son."

"Hutch, here's your chance. Might be your last chance. Go to the right place and you can retire."

"How much paper in that safe right now?"

"I told you. Almost a million dollars."

"Motherfucker, give me a real number. Not gonna put my life on the line for an 'almost.'"

"Okay, okay. Mr. C told the boss there was $982,300 in the safe. They were cleaning it out over the next couple days. In a month it'll be built up again. It's summer, but we're still pulling people in."

"You're straight with me on this?"

"Yeah, Hutch."

"Look here, bruh. I get half."

"Of course. I…"

"No, now you listen. I get half. Your dumb ass don't talk to nobody else 'bout this. I hear you do that or think you tryin' to play me, I put you down myself."

"Don't worry about it. With my mind and your muscles…"

"I said listen, motherfucker. Shit, *I* tell *you* how it's goin' down. Ain't gonna be no rinky dink plan. You know how I do. Methodical. You want me to mess with you on this, got to be on point. You fuck up, I go down too. We do this methodical, or we don't do it. I can live my life. Maintain like it has been. Alright."

"Yes, definitely."

"I wasn't askin'. That was me tellin' you how it is. Hear me?"

"Oh, I didn't…"

"Clint, shut the fuck up and listen. Placate me, motherfucker, alright. We do this in a month. Look up that date on your phone. Between now and then, this what happens. Empty bank accounts. Get rid of computers. No more Facebook and texting bullshit for you. Cut up credit cards. A week out, we get rid of our phones. You got a girlfriend? Roommate?"

"Negative on the roommate. Of course I got a girlfriend. And the date is the overnight of Saturday, June 7th and Sunday, June 8th."

"You don't say a word to her."

"No, don't worry."

"You don't say a word and you dump her tomorrow. Seriously. Don't do that and it's off. I'll take care of the getaway car and get us fake ID's. Passport for me. You want a passport?"

"No, I was thinking I'd go…"

"Stop! Don't tell me where you're goin'. I'm not tellin' you my place. When we leave the club, we drive straight to Houston. After that, we separate. Put some decoys in the trash at our places, throw 'em off track."

"Wow, Hutch. You definitely got your game face on."

"I invented the motherfuckin' game face. Hand me that egg roll."

"But tomorrow? I gotta break up with her tomorrow?"

"Yeah, and do it right quick."

"Okay…so the getaway car. What's it gonna be?"

"I don't know yet, Clint. Nothin' flashy. Anonymous. Wheels with a plate and a VIN that's not stolen and can't track to us."

"This isn't gonna be some rimmed out hooptie, is it, Hutch?"

"Rimmed out hooptie? That's some racist shit right there. Wrong decade too."

"Racist? I voted for Obama twice."

"I stand corrected. Racist and stupid, Clint. Racist and stupid."

"You're anti-Obama like the tea party nuts?"

"No, course not. Did I want the man in the office? Yeah. Am I glad you devils ain't killed him? Definitely. But, listen. I'm 16th Ward, born and raised. Forshey and Fern, near Earhart. What I know from all my years is don't trust a politician. Obama ain't Jesus. He's a politician. What's he done for me? I don't vote for none of 'em."

"But being black, you don't feel like you should…"

"So now you gonna tell me how I should be? I forgot. White's always right."

"That's not fair."

"You got that right. Not fair, but we livin' it. Matter fact, white means right and black means run, baby, run 'fore they get you. Now, enough of this nonsense. Don't look hurt, Clint. I ain't madatcha. It's on. Whatever you wanna call it – hit, heist, caper, robbery, rip-off – it's on."

Back to the present, Hutch sniffed and coughed from the mold. Remembering the hypothetical and living in the pragmatic was a big descent. It was a bad day. Luck couldn't get any worse. His walls had tumbled down. He hoped to fall asleep and not wake up. Let the mold overtake and turn him into organic matter like everything else in the place. Take the $1,200 in his pocket too. All he had left from the bank after expenses.

While Hutch was reaching needed slumber, three like-minded vehicles converged near him. One came from Broad, the second from Poydras, and the third from Espanade.

Each of them was driven by a black man in his 30's wearing tan work boots and an untucked uniform shirt over Dickies cargo pants. None of them worked for the same company.

Despite different starting points, they ended up in line on Claiborne before it became Robertson a few blocks from Elysian Fields. Each man was wondering which of the others was there to cheat him out of a pick-up. One of them, in fact, thought the two others were both there for that purpose All had Taurus .38 caliber revolvers in their glove boxes, but none wanted to use them. Their thoughts and mutterings were nearly identical.

"You think you're gonna step on me?"

"Nobody's steppin' on my pick-up."

"You better step off right now."

Frustration building, the men in the caravan of trucks were getting angrier at the unknown one playing dirty. None of them paid any notice to the rough looking young man carrying one crutch but walking fine on Elysian Fields.

All antagonism melted away, though, once two of the trucks turned on Franklin toward the flashing lights and first responders in the intersection to pick up a Honda Civic and a jeep.

The remaining driver continued on Robertson until he got to Piety. A few neighbors were outside, looking at the corner house with an SUV sized hole in it. The residents of the house were still hunkered down because of Johnny rolling down his car window and announcing that he'd put a bigger hole in anyone who came up to the front room.

The driver attached his winch, Johnny and Big T got out and scaled the remnants of the former rooms, and they met the tow truck driver.

"What's up, Melvin? Thanks for taking care of the predicament," Johnny said in a way to act like he wasn't in a ridiculous situation. "Mr. C will take care of you for flying out here right away."

3

The images in a nicely framed poster of the *Donald Byrd and 125th St., N.Y.C.* album cover were in sharp contrast to what lay a few feet below. In Ernie Barnes' inimitable artwork, elongated bodies did their thing on the dance floor to the groove played by five musicians on stage. Those up in the cheap seats shook and raised their hands to the sky. Energy personified.

The poster was the only thing up on the walls of the apartment. Everything else was in boxes stacked throughout a few of the six rooms. The renter of the apartment and owner of these items, the one who wanted the poster up if nothing else yet, was stretched out on a mattress and springs on the floor.

His name was Bobby Delery.

Delery had gotten to town the day before, after driving down from Chicago. He'd taken a midway break in Memphis to stretch the trip into two days and see the Stax Museum. The U-Haul truck he drove had a trailer on back for his car.

He knew it was bad judgment to leave anything in the truck overnight in New Orleans, so he'd unloaded it all himself while listening to WWOZ streaming on his laptop computer. It was his first time back in over thirty years.

After a day of driving and moving in by himself, Delery was aching and bone-tired. He'd fallen asleep quickly. No nightmares, which came far too often in his line of work, though it was typically in an academic setting.

Bobby Delery was a criminologist. He'd been on faculty at the University of Chicago for years but had a new position at Tulane.

His phone started ringing. Simple tone. Nothing fancy or personalized.

Delery yawned, squinted his eyes open, and picked up the phone. 7:28 a.m. on a Sunday morning. The numbers following the 504 area code weren't his landlord's. He was of a mind to let it go to voice mail, but he was a professional, so he decided otherwise and cleared his throat before answering.

"This is Bobby Delery," he said in a parched and strained rasp.

The responding voice was of different timbre. Wide awake. Thick. Sharp.

"This is Commander Edwin Jones of the 5th District. Are you in town, Delery? You awake?"

The general black New Orleans cadence was a beautiful thing. Despite being woken up, Delery felt home already. His soul rode the waves of inflection, even Jones' severe sounding version.

"Yes sir, I am. On both counts. But I'm a little confused by the call," Delery said.

"I bet you are. Let's straighten that out," Jones replied. "Chief Stewart passed on your phone number. I know you just arrived, but we have a situation."

"I spoke with him last week. Has something changed with the working relationship I'll have with NOPD?" Delery asked, thinking of his recent conversation with Police Chief Louis Stewart.

"Let me cut to the chase, then we'll work back. We'd greatly appreciate it if that working relationship started today."

In a flash, Delery thought about what he'd planned to have his day consist of. First, go out and have breakfast. Next, drive over to the West Bank and pick out a refrigerator to get delivered. The previous tenant took the one that was there when moving out, and the landlord was renting the place as is. Beginning the task of unpacking would follow. At least he could get a start on all this before meeting with NOPD.

"Okay, where's the best place to get together after lunch? For lunch if you want."

"Delery, when I say 'start today,' let me amend that to 'start immediately.' We've got a serious matter, and I think you have a unique perspective to offer," Jones said.

"Commander, right now?" Delery was surprised. As a criminologist, he'd typically consulted with CPD in Chicago to help identify patterns of behavior by criminals or speak on current theories and studies that were relevant. Typical scheduling was involved. He'd not heard about anything particularly pressing in New Orleans, like a serial killer on the loose.

Jones spoke with reluctance. "Yes, right now we're playing catch up. I suppose you haven't seen the news yet?"

"No sir," Delery answered.

"We have a situation. Media anymore, they all take something and run with it. A reporter for NOLA.com, one of these new kids they keep hiring from out of state – nothing personal – was having himself a party with friends late night on Bourbon Street. Place called Club Big Easy. He overhears the manager all frantic that they'd been robbed. So this guy… let me see here..this guy name of Joseph Bomar posts the story online from the club. Somehow it gets okayed or never got approval. Goes online. Shouldn't be a problem, right? Who's reading the news then? Well, that's what I thought. But it starts making the rounds. Infernal social media. The word gets spread. There's no Sunday morning news shows on tv, but they all posted it on their websites too. Now we got a shitstorm."

"Because it's not true?" Delery asked.

"No, problem is that it *is* true and now it's out there. It's a million dollars true. We've got to act fast," Jones said.

"A million dollar robbery?" Delery questioned.

"Uh huh. Here's where it gets down and dirty. The club

that got hit is one of…uh, it's owned by a man you don't rob. Enough said? He *will* have his boys take care of things. We need to find the perps first. It'll look bad otherwise. Already started," Jones answered.

"But what can I do? And what happened?"

"Delery, a body's been found. They pretty much crucified the guy on a guard rail. Chief can't have a bloodbath in the city. We need to find the others and clean this up. Must've been a crew."

Delery was in a quandary. He knew NOPD was short-staffed, precariously so, and suspected they were merely wanting to use him as an extra body to investigate. He wondered if his newly-retired predecessor at Tulane, Steven Sharp, had been asked to take on this kind of thing. If Delery said yes now, it wouldn't stop.

"Sir, can I have a minute?" he asked.

"Of course," Jones replied.

Delery rose from his makeshift bed, phone still in hand. He scratched his stomach with the other hand. Now that he was up, he stood at a full 5'10", lean but lightly muscular from working out twice a week. 160 lbs, give or take, ever since high school. He had a slightly swarthy complexion, which often led people to think his ethnic background was Jewish or Italian, though he was neither. His black hair was fine of texture but tended to turn curly once it got a little long, as it was on the verge of. Delery walked through the kitchen and took a sip of water, spilling a little on his gym shorts and Curtom Records t-shirt.

He thought, "If I give in now, already, I'll keep getting treated like a sucker. This isn't how I'm to help them out. Media interviews, trainings, discussions, working up profiles of offenders, sure. Not this."

But he also considered why he became a criminologist.

Genuinely wondering what made people tick. When that psychology was extended into actions that occurred despite social mores and laws, the hidden human emerged. He only experienced this by way of books and statistics, though.

Then it clicked. A feeling of confidence rose in him.

"Commander?"

Jones, hearing the change in Delery's voice, assumed the worst.

"Delery, I should tell you that Chief Stewart has read all your books. You've impressed him. He's convinced that with your assistance we can wrap this up and apprehend all the remaining perps before it gets ugly in public."

Delery appreciated the ego stroke. Though it was obvious, the gesture might've pushed him toward a "yes" if he'd been about to say the opposite. He didn't have his masters in criminology, but being published was the great equalizer.

"Commander, I'll head out in a minute, but here's what I need. By evening, if not before, an NOPD van takes me over the river to Sears, J.C. Penney, whichever. I pick out a refrigerator, they load it up, bring it to my place, and inside to the kitchen. They'll need a sturdy hand cart, I expect."

Jones paused and responded strongly, "Yes, sure, we can do that. My word on it."

Delery shook his head sagely. Back home and already in the groove. Scratch my back, I scratch yours. Take care of me, I take care of you. Establish right off that he knew how the game was played.

"Sounds good. So where do I start?" Delery asked, hoping it was near a place where he could get the cup of coffee he desperately needed.

After Commander Jones briefed him, Delery sighed.

"How am I going to find something to wear in here?" he said to the surrounding mess.

He was a sound believer in first impressions, so dressed as he was, or wearing the green camouflage shorts he'd had on yesterday wouldn't fly. All his other clothes would be at least partly wrinkled. Little chance of locating the iron.

When he'd moved in the past, even little cross-town moves in Chicago, he'd been careful to label boxes with a marker. Not this time. Delery had expected to have a week of unpacking, acclimating, and getting his office in order. He'd figured that was a good amount of time, considering that early June temperatures were already in the upper 90's. The pace of things in New Orleans can be attributed in part to a climate of a solid five to six summer months.

"At least I know where this is," Delery said, picking up his utility knife from the kitchen counter. The knife was his method of opening boxes, so he'd not packed it. For safety along the way too.

Delery was at a loss for which boxes to try first to locate a simple shirt and pants suitable for both summer and a decent appearance. The only boxes he knew to avoid were the larger wooden ones that contained his records, over half of them inherited from his father. The rest collected over the last couple years. Up to at least 500.

With only a few exceptions, they were all from the 70's. Mostly the first half. That sweet soul sound of classic r&b and funk, plus its confluence with jazz.

"Wow, these records back in New Orleans with me. I'd be an easy read for a psych analysis."

Delery was a few months from turning 44. Born in 1970. His dad was a music buff. The kind who tsk-tsk'ed with his eyes, if not verbally expressing disapproval when turning off his son's music in apartment or car. Same thing said each time.

It came down to, "I can't listen to this. No warmth."

Delery knew what was meant about both music and cd's.

He'd been close enough to his dad to understand shorthand. Past tense anyway. George Delery had a fatal heart attack over three years ago. Mama and his brothers gone too.

Bobby Delery had no more immediate family and didn't know his extended family. None of them came to Dad's funeral anyway.

Moving past the records and on to potential boxes of clothing, Delery recalled his dad's last week and a certain request repeated at least once each day in a voice barely above a whisper.

"Bobby. Bobby. Don't sell my records, son. Keep 'em 'til you need 'em."

His dad knew him. "Dusty" and "old school" were the pleasant pejoratives Delery had thought to himself.

But then they sat. Lined the walls of his apartment. His plan had been to wait a month and sell them at the record store on Ashland.

Barely a week after the funeral, though, he could hardly stand the untidiness. He went over to a random pile, stacked up a couple feet high. Flipping through them, he came to the batch of Donald Byrd. At least a dozen. He hadn't actively seen these covers in years, but they jolted him as if common DNA.

Delery took one out, *Places and Spaces* by Byrd, that seemed to resonate more than the others. He impulsively tucked the record under his arm and headed out to the electronics store a few blocks away. It was an odd arrival, but without specific details he explained to the clerk that he needed to briefly use a record player.

The high school student didn't mind, because she didn't care one way or the other what happened there. Delery was embarrassed to find that he didn't know how to use the record player other than setting its speed to 33 rpm.

When he finally figured it out, he sat dumbstruck and was

transported to his childhood. This was the soundtrack to his memories. The first few years of his life staying on the corner of Galvez and Poland.

He was midway between nine and ten years old when his parents divorced. It was acrimonious. His dad was given custody of him, while Mama got his two younger brothers in the proceedings.

A person can stay in New Orleans yet just about disappear from friends by moving across town. His dad instead took him and lit out for an entirely different territory. Indiana. Young Bobby never saw his mama again. Isaac and Curtis either.

Those were the thoughts that shook his bones as he sat there, listening through the headphones. So much had passed.

Delery saw the musical chain unveil before his eyes of everything he'd been into, whether temporary or enduring. Pop radio, hip hop, hair metal, alternative, indie, South American folk, Eastern European brass, and much more. But now he was sonically back home.

He began building stackable wooden boxes for the records that same weekend. It all was most likely the catalyst for his eventual return to New Orleans.

Once he made up his mind, Delery checked and found that both Albert Olivier at SUNO and Steven Sharp at Tulane were the criminologists of note in the city, and men in their 60's. He sent them both emails and called to follow up. Although Olivier was holding on a little while longer, Sharp was planning to retire, and he put in a good word with the university brass.

All this and more ran through Delery's mind while he sliced through the packing tape securing seven boxes before discovering suitable but wrinkled clothing. Dark blue light-weight button-up shirt, grey pleated and cuffed dress pants, black oxfords.

"At least my shoes don't need shined," he rued, unfolding

and shaking the outfit. "Not a good first impression, but it's my current situation."

Delery scooped up the few items needed for the day: his shoulder bag, notebook and a couple pens, the sun protection he'd kept out during the moving drive, a full 20 ounce bottle of water, and the utility knife just in case. Coffee would need to be found on the way there.

4

Delery stepped out of the Burger King at the foot of Robertson, right before it gradually rose to its elevated section. Desperate times, desperate measures, so the coffee would have to do. No way he'd touch the food, though.

He was parked with the cluster of squad cars right off Franklin, out of the way of oncoming traffic, but before two blue and whites turned sideways to block further ascent. Looking up the incline, he saw EMS, coroner's van, and a city vehicle.

Delery had read the 2011 Justice Department report released as the initial investigative part of the consent decree. Mayor Walter Vaccaro campaigned on cleaning up NOPD and invited in the feds, but he quickly reversed and spent hundreds of thousands of public dollars in legal fees fighting it.

The consent decree was happening, though.

Delery recalled the report as a severe evaluation that touched on unconstitutionality and major deficiencies across every aspect of policing. Use of force; general stops, searches, and arrests; discrimination; policies; recruitment; training and supervision; details, the supposed to be off-the-clock security jobs; evaluations and promotions; misconduct; and more.

It was no wonder crime levels were worsening. Despite some good officers, NOPD was often brutal and sloppy. A former colleague coined the term "malicious incompetence," and Delery thought that likely summed it up fairly well. New Orleans had a crime problem, but a broken police force didn't help.

Delery had no I.D. other than his Illinois driver's license and was an unknown, so the uniform standing between the two horizontally turned cars called to confirm access.

"Alright, you're good," the young cop said, chewing his gum.

Walking up the incline, Delery knew he was intruding on a place where everyone had their roles, cops and criminals both. He was invited to the dance, but it didn't mean a thing.

He couldn't help but be struck by the view. It reminded him of how he felt driving in on I-10 yesterday as it swooped into the downtown rooftops and cemeteries. In this case, a long train yard.

The EMS personnel were leaving since the body was clearly deceased. Two coroners were in the process of slowly prying a body from the guard rail it was fused to. The back of the corpse faced everyone else. One coroner held the upper body from the right side to keep the head and arms from slumping over the top while the other coroner pried from the left with what looked like a polite crowbar. A gurney sat empty at their feet.

"This is slow going. Nasty shit. We've got skin and a few internal organs coming loose. He's stuck to the metal," one of them called out to the array.

In a loose semi-circle around the body, two white shirts were in conversation, a couple casual but professionally dressed detectives were walking around separately, and a crime scene technician was taking photos of an overturned beige sofa that had a small orange-red rubber cone placed next to it. The cone read "1." A couple more evidence cones were in place.

On the periphery of the crime scene, a group of other first responders was casually chatting or tapping on their phones.

Everyone up there with Delery was male, except for one EMT and the technician shooting photos.

Delery approached the white shirts, directly facing the one who seemed to be in command. He quickly scanned the pockmarked man's star and crescent for confirmation.

"Yes, the captain," Delery observed. "P. Connell" was the

name engraved on the brass name tag.

Captain Connell looked at his lieutenant, a light-skinned black man with freckled cheeks and reddish hair, then at his watch. Both could only be physically described as ample.

They knew who Delery was and why he was there before he extended his hand and introduced himself. The college egghead. And they had to make nice, to a certain extent.

Connell enveloped Delery's hand with a firm grip and fingers that felt like fingerling potatoes. He was spud-like in other ways too. Nose like a russet. Mouth like a yam. Ears like Yukon Golds. Eyelids like French fries. All of them the consistency of red potatoes getting redder while standing in full-on sun.

His demeanor was also starchy.

"We've been expecting you, Delery. Captain Patrick Connell's my name. This is Lieutenant James Alvar. You've been sleeping in your clothes. It's 8 'o clock on the dot. We've been working. Looks like a 30." Connell was testing him.

"Captain, I just got to town. The wrinkled clothes are only my current situation. Otherwise, I'd…"

"Save it."

"Sir, when you say 'a 30,' is that NOPD's code for homicide 1st degree? CPD, uh in Chicago, used 110."

"Delery, this isn't Chicago. No, they say New Orleans is progressing. Progress is bleeding us dry, but progress it is. Regardless, here's what I need from you. Witnesses. Find them. Somebody out there saw something," he said, gesturing to the patchwork of train tracks, warehouses, empty lots, and houses below, leading to the river.

"Sir, Commander Jones said the vic is connected to a major robbery. How do we know that?"

"How do we know? Number one, the vic's wearing his Club Big Easy shirt. Partly anyway. Same place that was robbed.

He was seen working bar last night. Two, his wallet contains a Louisiana driver's license in the name of Clint Olson. That one's legitimate. We've checked."

Connell wiped his brow. "Also has a California license in the name of Paul Grayson. That's the fake. Nothing else in the wallet. No credit cards. Nothing. Except for a couple thousand in cash. No phone either. He was keeping lean to get away. Or the men connected to his employer grabbed everything else. Either way he's connected."

"What about the couch? Could this have been a hit and run?"

"Do you know how many junk collectors drive around in rickety trucks full of crap, none of it secured? It's coincidental. No, Delery. What I see is a statement. They caught Olson, brought him out here, threatened to throw him over if he didn't talk, blowtorched his guts, and stuck him on the guard rail as an example to the rest of Olson's crew. Not that we can prove any of that."

"But sir…"

"Witnesses, Delery, witnesses," Connell thundered, before looking over at Alvar and dryly dropping, "He's lucky he doesn't have FIC's."

Delery excused himself and stepped away from the two men, understanding more than they thought. It was obvious to him that none of the others were about to walk down Robertson, loop around and under on the surface roads, trudging around in the heat and catching hell for waking people up on a Sunday morning. They had their narrative wrapped up. But how was it a path forward to solving the crime?

He also knew what FIC's were. Field Interview Cards. A key part of Chief Stewart's statistics-driven approach. According to the fed's report, officers were spending time on FIC quotas instead of policing.

Delery was unaware that NOPD had already put out an alert for witnesses in the vicinity to contact them immediately. He passed the two detectives conferring. They gave him blank looks with flashes of smugness, knowing he was on the way to do their job.

"I'll learn from this. There's something more to it," he emphasized to himself.

He was barely past them when one of the detectives made no effort to conceal his complaint. "The homies can shoot each other all day long, but I put a bullet in one of them, and it's the end of the fucking world."

Delery's heart sunk. The consent decree report again. Officers involved in shootings were temporarily assigned to the Homicide Division as a matter of practice so that their statements were effectively immunized. Actual investigations of the shootings were thus neutralized. And it was still happening.

"What the hell am I doing here? This isn't my home anymore. If I was in Chicago right now, I know exactly what I'd be doing. It wouldn't be this," he muttered to himself.

The young officer serving as sentry greeted Delery back at the surface road.

"Connell call you out on the wrinkled clothes?"

"Normally I wouldn't be looking like this, but yes he did," Delery admitted, being kind enough not to comment that the rookie's uniform blues were a size too large.

"Learn from it all, Bobby," he added to himself.

Instead of taking the quick route, he followed Port down a block before making one left back into the neighborhood and another to complete the horseshoe and find himself back where he'd started, but twenty feet below.

Immediately upon turning off of Villere onto St. Ferdinand, he'd trained his gaze upward on the coroners working away to loosen the body of Clint Olson from the guard rail so he could get the neighbors' perspective on the scene. He'd kept to the left side of the street and on the sidewalk until it disappeared and became a grassy graveled path.

Though it didn't look like a good area for witnesses, what with so much of it uninhabited and the homicide taking place out of eyesight, he thought it best to start under where it all happened and work his way from house to house.

Delery turned, the crime scene now just behind him, and took a few steps. His mouth opened slightly, he nodded in realization, and moved forward a bit more. He turned and faced upward.

"Get Captain Connell. There's blood here. A trail of it too," he yelled.

A few seconds later, the captain peered over the guard rail. He wasn't in the mood to be bothered.

"What is it, Delery?"

"Captain, there's a little pool of blood here. It trails off toward the neighborhood."

The reply was not at all what he anticipated.

"Of course there's blood down there. Plenty of blood up here too. The vic's leaned over a guard rail. Some of it dripped down."

"But sir, there's no spatter here. If it was dripping from up there, don't you think it'd look differently down here?"

"You know, I expected more from you. One of two things is clear. Number one, the vic's bleeding out, some falls below, and an animal walks through it, spreading the trail. There are strays all over the place. Two, there's no connection with that blood and the vic's. Look where you're standing. Custom made spot for a drug deal gone bad. Probably one of the train hoppers who think this city is Mayberry with better music. Trust me, no connection."

"Sir, with all due respect, this seems…"

"You just got to town, Delery. It might surprise you, but down here in the South, we do know a few things."

"I'm a native New Orleanian, but that's beside the point."

Connell erupted.

"Goddamn, Delery. Have you thought through the narrative you're spinning? Either the vic is up here, he drips, and the blood tip toes down the street, or they pull the guy dripping away and hoist him up here. Maybe in this fine piece of furniture. Those scenarios sound probable to you? My men put that kind of malarkey in a report, I'd tear it up. Your teaching have that lack of rigor? The commander promised you'd be a credit, but it's not looking like that. My technician is staying up here where she's got work to do. I don't want to hear another word of it."

At that he turned and vanished from sight. Delery was astonished, both at the tongue-lashing he'd received and that potential evidence was so blatantly ignored.

He realized why he ultimately said yes to Commander Jones. Theories, stats, and lecterns were his world. He craved stepping out of it and into the street, testing his mettle. It was intoxicating. And he knew there was something to what he'd discovered.

He muttered, "Is Connell only after a tidy report? Doesn't want the rest of the vic's crew found? The money too. The captain isn't lax, so the question is who he's really working for."

The call from the commander was ordered by Chief Stewart. It wouldn't have been made otherwise. Something wasn't quite right, though, and it picked at him.

For now, he had blood to follow. Conveniently it led toward the people to interview, but the houses didn't begin until over halfway through the block.

So much graffiti in this area. The figure he'd just seen on the support column. All the rusted out ramshackle buildings on either side of the train tracks covered with it. None of it very interesting. Common.

Delery stayed off to the side of the sporadic dried blood trail.

The first house he came to had a hippie van with Vermont plates parked in front. Weeds were overgrown and hemming in the house on both sides. Little items like beer bottles, crawfish shells, an old Atari joystick, and random pieces of wadded up clothing dotted the exterior ground. Banana trees barely taller than the weeds separated the house from its boarded-up neighbor.

His notebook and pen were at the ready. Closest riverside house to the crime scene. Delery suspected the inhabitants didn't go to bed early.

The door and two windows had colorful handmade art objects hanging from the outside. Privacy wasn't provided by curtains.

Delery knew blocks like this, where no one had curtains, at least those formally labeled as such. Instead, these people, like so many others, make do. They use a bed sheet, bath towel, tin foil, long skirt, military surplus blanket, or maybe a beach towel redeemed from collecting Marlboro Miles. He'd even seen an old rug used, apparently nailed up to hold its weight. They make do.

Delery knocked twice firmly, stepped back down off of the stoop, and took one more step back for good measure.

"People rarely come knocking here," he thought. "Door's as likely to be answered by somebody with a gun as not answered at all."

He understood it, though. Self preservation. The type of defensive living many people have no idea exists. An environment where you have to be continually on your guard from those who want to pick your bones or smash them up.

In New Orleans neighborhoods like this one, gun ownership

was a given for precisely this reason. Not for political nonsense or to do anyone harm. Merely to protect what was yours, and that included the lives of your family.

Delery himself wasn't a gun owner, saw no need, and planned to leave his utility knife tucked away, but he grew up in a similar block. Not quite as rough looking, but one where he quickly learned the rules.

He knew he no longer had the remnant of any New Orleans accent. The flat Midwesternese of Fort Wayne followed by the crisp Chicago version had taken care of that. Delery was fully aware that he looked wrinkled and sounded like an outsider. He relished getting his hands dirty though, so he was ready to dive in.

The slightest of cracks appeared, only enough to allow a shaggy blond head to peek out from the door. "Yeah?" called out a voice with layers of nicotine and cheap booze pasted to it.

"Ma'am, sorry to disturb you. My name's Bobby Delery. I'm assisting the police with a homicide that happened overnight up there on the overpass," he replied, gesturing with a glance.

"Oh. We didn't see nothin', if that's what you're wonderin'."

"It's possible you heard or even saw something important that doesn't seem pertinent."

Delery recalled the coroner's banter.

"Probably happened over two hours ago. Were you awake at that time?"

The door opened wider as a tough-eyed man wearing only blue jeans said, "Whozit, Mez?"

She was now exposed in a long skirt and flimsy blouse. Her full head of hair was in contrast to his shortly-cropped version. Both looked tan from outside work and worn from leisure.

Delery repeated himself. All of them stayed standing as is.

The man picked at his goatee and announced, "I'm Leonard. This is Mezzanine. We're kinda on a date. Not in touch with the outside world, if you know what I mean."

Before Delery could respond, the man anticipated him. "Don't mind you askin', but we got nothin' for you. Just my new girlfriend and me enjoyin' ourselves. I appreciate you gettin' to the point concisely, though. Gotdamn adverbs. Too many people use 'em." With that, he nodded and ducked back inside.

"Thank you anyway, sir. Ma'am. Thanks for your time," Delery said.

Mezzanine took a break from biting her lip and said, "He's my ex-husband. Maybe second time's a charm."

Delery went back to following the blood trail down the block.

A pick-up truck ambled along, odd in a fairly solitary place. It stopped. The driver was a narrow headed burr cut man with a quizzical face.

"What's goin' on up there?" he asked, looking ahead. The coroners turned, having at last removed the body from the guard rail.

Before Delery could respond, the man lifted his left hand. "Nah, I can guess. That's how those people wanna live."

Anger drew up from inside Delery. He could feel it smearing his face.

"Those people? That's a dead white guy up there. Probably killed by white guys. Those the people you're talking about?"

He caught himself from going any further. "Don't say it. This isn't personal. All you'd do is surprise him. No benefit," he privately cautioned.

"You can say what you want, but I just work here. Lay my head down in Chalmette. Much safer there," the man said with a confused scowl that labeled Delery a traitor, and drove off.

Bobby Delery had seen that look before. Too often, in fact. He knew it was best to let it go and only play his trump card if absolutely necessary. It was an odd trump card, though.

He also knew that the murder rate in New Orleans, though dropping the past few years, had been at military-zone levels for quite some time. Life was cheap. Mainly for black men. Kids too. The ones killing them were their black brothers. Over 90% of the killing in New Orleans. Nationally, at eight times the rate of white folks. All of them pawns. They'd internalized the hatred and were now the death makers of their own kind. Self-lynchers.

As he continued on, he heard his name yelled behind him. Captain Connell.

He walked back to the overpass, feeling sweat cloaking him all over.

"Delery, Detectives Bergeron and Taylor are on their way to canvass the houses and businesses lakeside of the overpass. Email me if you get anything," Connell said, before tossing down his business card and walking off.

Delery realized he'd been shunted off to where the closest potential witness was half a block away, leaving the quality interviews for the detectives. They'd get those who lived steps from the overpass or had an upper window view, like that tall art gallery building. Assuming those interviews were actually happening.

He refused to feel defeated, though. The blood trail meant something.

As he headed back down the street to continue his own interviews, the cacophony of several voices rose behind him. Loudest was the captain's.

"Goddamn it. Stop that gurney."

Delery could tell from the direction of the heads bobbing in desperation that the gurney with the body of Clint Olson strapped to it was flying down the incline toward Franklin, picking up speed by the second.

5

The internal alarm clock rang in the sleeping soul of Melba Barnes at 8:37 a.m. She was a retired woman in her late 60's living alone. Her days were organized around the timekeeper that didn't tick, beep, chime, or play the snippet of a song. When it said "hungry," she ate and "tired," she slept.

It was Sunday, which meant she had one ongoing appointment. Church.

She sat up in bed after making sure her satin hair bonnet was still in place. It was necessary to protect her hair after moisturizing and sealing it at the end of the night.

In immediate response, two cats stretched to life in slow motion from their curled-up positions. Time for breakfast.

"Good morning, Too-too. Moses."

She'd had Moses for years. One night, the wooded area near the house caught fire and she'd seen the little orange cat high-tailing it out of there. Her husband Alvin prompted the name when he said, "Look at that cat come out the burning bush!"

The younger feline, also a stray, was one who showed up outside last year. It had a patchwork of color and what resembled a nicely groomed moustache. Miss Melba thought he looked like legendary musician Allen Toussaint, what with the dignified moustache, soulful eyes, and four brown paws that had a few inches of white fur above them. Socks with sandals a la Toussaint were what she saw. Stylishly handsome too.

She'd prayed about it, if it was indecent to bring another man into her house, another man's name even, when Alvin was barely dead in the ground. The answer, not surprisingly, was affirmative that this was no issue.

If five more strays had shown up in the meantime, Miss Melba would've taken each of them in too. Alvin only liked one cat underfoot, but without him around and her children away in far-flung places, she felt a calling.

Tenisha taught history at Boston College, Aspen was a medical doctor in Oakland, and her baby Ezekiel was the Senior Curator of Visual Arts at the Walker Art Center in Minneapolis.

"Raise them up, and they'll go to the three corners," she often thought. "Alvin with the Sewerage & Water Board and me at the hotel all those years, but look at the kids."

Miss Melba's morning routine began with feeding the cats, taking a carton of milk from the refrigerator, wrapping up in a robe and donning her eyeglasses, stepping out on the porch to collect the newspaper, and boiling water to make café au lait for sipping while she read the news and obituaries.

This morning she had a surprise.

"Oh. Mercy, what is this?" she cried out. She tightened her robe and took another tentative step, ready to dash back inside.

Alongside her house, between it and an empty lot that led to a few trees, was a man on the ground. He was face down. His large backpack was squarely in place and partially obscuring a sizable colorful box.

She took another step, expecting him to pop up at any moment and grab at her. Miss Melba paused. All was well so far. Two more steps. This led her to the side end of the porch. She leaned over the iron rail.

There was something next to him she'd not initially seen. It looked like a mouse or small rodent was sticking out from under his head.

"Oh my goodness. On Sunday morning," she said.

Miss Melba took a few steps back and picked up the clay flower pot from its stand. The prickly leaves of a bromeliad scratched her wrists.

She slowly moved from the porch to the steps, craning her head to make sure the figure wasn't moving. The other houses on her dead end street had either been torn down or were still blighted, except for one. A neighbor she didn't care for.

Creeping down the steps and around the house, Miss Melba felt like she was in a monster movie. She inched closer, raising the flower pot up as a weapon in case the zombie rose to life and attacked her. When she was steps away, she realized that this was the whitest white man she'd ever seen.

"He's the color of toothpaste," she said.

As she stood beside the figure, she saw another small hairy rodent poking out from the other side of his head. She leaned in, peering intently at this alien creature. It was then Miss Melba realized that the two mice were the two ends of his shaggy moustache.

"It's not at all a nicely cultivated one like Allen Toussaint's. Man or cat," she said.

She was further bewildered by the box, a mélange of purple, brown, reddish-brown, and white colors, until she saw it from its longer side.

"Abita Amber," she read and saw the accompanying beer bottles pictured.

"Hmph. He's just a passed out drunk."

She thought for a quick moment and decided to help him. He was a stray, after all.

Miss Melba walked with purpose back up to the porch and planted the flowerpot right back in its proper place. She was no longer worried about being attacked but remained cautious.

"I'm gonna help you kick that habit," she said.

She walked over to the beer case and picked it up, immediately straining from the weight. The pieces of the lid were twisted together in an alternating way to keep the case firmly closed.

"My goodness. Beer's gotten so heavy. Must be all the sin in it."

She'd had a sip of Budweiser once in high school and found it as appetizing as water from a rusty tin can. Never touched it since.

Miss Melba walked to her house and up the steps, pushed her front door with a foot, and stepped inside. She immediately sat the box down, then turned and locked the door once it was hastily closed. She'd eventually take some coffee out to the comatose drunkard, but right now she had the Lord's work to do. Everything else was secondary.

She lifted her weighty burden and carried it past the little church organ. Past all the framed pictures on the walls and tops of cabinets and mantles. Aspen with his high school diploma, looking serious as always. Tenisha's 10th birthday party back when she was all braids and eyelashes. Alvin holding up the biggest redfish he ever caught. Ezekiel standing proudly next to a painting at the McKenna Museum.

She continued through the kitchen. A row of canisters tidily lined the back counter. Postcards from around the world draped across the refrigerator.

After a couple steps down the hallway, passing the cat food and water bowls, she turned into the bathroom and set the case down next to the toilet. A manual can opener and roll of paper towels were retrieved from the kitchen and a large trash bag from the storage room.

Miss Melba put the items down, and seeing no better place, sat on the closed toilet to pray for Jesus' blessing of her actions. When she finished, she stood and lifted the lid.

"Only good place for this booze," she said.

Her plan was to open each beer bottle, one at a time, pour its contents into the commode, and wrap it with a couple paper towels before finally depositing it into the trash bag. Miss Melba didn't want to allow any possibility for the trash men to hear the bottles and think her a lush.

Small narrow fingers pulled the four parts of the lid loose so that they all flipped up and opened together. While reaching with her other hand for the opener, she dove in for the first bottle and was shocked when her fingers didn't brush up against glass or metal.

"Oh my!" she exclaimed.

Her hand pulled back as if she'd mistakenly touched the thorns of a rose bush.

Miss Melba dropped the can opener so that both hands could slowly pull the pieces of lid back further and she could look inside. Her eyes popped. Pupils and irises became ink blots in a sea of milk.

"Aaaaah," she said in an orgasmically alarmed way from the roof of her mouth. Her jaw dropped.

She reached in with both hands and took out a bound packet of money. Next the one below it. And the following.

Miss Melba didn't stop until the bathroom floor was covered with the contents.

She flipped through one crisp packet, saw each top left-hand corner had a small dot from a highlighter pen, and did the mathematics in her head. She extended an index finger and counted the total number of packets around her.

Furrowing her brow, she started again through the numbers. They were correct the first time. $10,000 per packet. Ninety-seven packets. She was surrounded by nearly a million dollars.

"Sweet Jesus," she said in amazement. She studied the money and thought. Then she thought some more until she had a plan for what to do.

Miss Melba rose and stepped over and through the money.

She closed the toilet lid and sat on it.

"Lord, come back. Don't go away. I really need you now."

A swollen five minutes passed before Miss Melba stood up, collected the money packets, all with a large "100" in each corner and a pursed-lip Benjamin Franklin staring at her, placed them back into the beer case, and folded the top pieces to secure it.

She made another cup of coffee, poured it into Alvin's old mug, and carried it to the front.

"Keep me protected," she said as she unlocked the door and stepped past it onto the porch.

The comatose man was nowhere to be seen. "Oh!" she cried out, worried that he was up and dangerous. A little coffee spilled. She crept to the rail and peered over, then crossed the porch to the other side.

"No sign of him," she said. Miss Melba went back to the front door, locked it, and put the keys in her robe's front pocket.

"Not decent to be out like this, but I did it once already, so here we go."

She took the steps down and slowly walked around her house clockwise, keeping a wide berth. "Ooooo," she said in a low nervous voice the whole way around.

Back at the front steps. He was gone.

Miss Melba looked upward. "My goodness, I doubted You. That won't happen twice." The reply was unexpected. "A sacred Sunday to you, Sister Barnes."

Miss Melba jumped with surprise and spilled the remaining coffee to the ground. "I…I…how long have you been standing there?" she asked.

"I rose only minutes ago," he said from the house across the street and over one lot.

It looked it. The man, her only Industrial Court neighbor, was wrapped in a purple sheet, not immodestly. He was covered from ankles to neck, with long dreadlocks spilling down to his stomach.

Still, Miss Melba didn't know him that way.

"Oh. Well, I was blessing the house. The perimeter. But I shouldn't be out like this." With that, she scurried back inside as quickly as her old legs could handle.

He kept his gaze fixed with eyes that some had known as beatific and others as malevolent over the years.

Miss Melba knew him as Claude Collins from Kenosha, Wisconsin. The mailman whispered that to her shortly after the stranger moved in a few months ago.

Most of his mail came addressed to Hawk Anderson, though. When they'd initially met, he introduced himself to her as a direct descendent of Mother Leafy Anderson and Black Hawk.

Miss Melba had been attending more mainstream churches her whole life, but she knew what he was referencing. Anderson, who claimed to commune with Midwestern Native American war leader Black Hawk, was the woman behind the New Orleans Spiritualist churches back in the 1920's.

Collins was typically decked out in a top hat, head scarf, and long embroidered robe when he left the house, though he rarely did. Multiple bead necklaces and bracelets of all colors accentuated the picture.

Like all New Orleanians, Miss Melba appreciated style and panache, but she also had a saying, "Too much flash is trash."

When she told Tenisha about the new neighbor during one of their phone conversations, her daughter immediately looked him up on her computer.

"Mother, listen to what I found. Houseoftheholyhawk.com He's got a website with pictures and a list of his fees. Here's an amulet. 'Voodoo protection. Keeps the haters away.' He takes money orders, credit cards, Paypal, you name it."

"But baby, I don't see him come and go much, less it's at night. People either."

"Here's why. He charges less if the consultations are by email or letter. Listen to this. 'My guidance replies are learned, blessed, and individualized from the True Way. They are also in Times New Roman font at 14 point and double-spaced.' Hawk charges for 'emergency texting if in spiritual crisis.' A charlatan. Probably harmless, though."

"Don't you worry 'bout me, 'Nisha. Your mama keeps to herself."

Miss Melba had all of this in mind when she walked through the house and back to the bathroom to double-check that the money was still there.

"Look at me. Old fool running for money that's not even mine," she said.

Moses was rubbing his head against the beer case. Allen Toussaint calmly sat on top of it.

"Moses, my baby, you are something else. It's not food. Too-too, always a gentleman."

Miss Melba walked back to the bedroom and across to the dresser on the opposite side of the room. It hadn't been opened for a while, so the handles were a little dusty. She pulled open the lower right-hand drawer and rummaged through Alvin's athletic clothing until she found a carrying case about a foot long.

After flipping the clasp and opening the case, she ran her fingers along a black metal object and lifted it from the surrounding foam.

"Hasn't been shot off since Zekey was in high school," she recalled.

It probably wouldn't be needed, but just in case. She held it out in front of her, walked it to the built-in closet, and gently placed it in her largest purse, which was white.

"That just determined my wardrobe for church," she said.

Miss Melba typically arrived at The Tab by 11:00 a.m., but she knew the weight of the beer case would slow her usual half hour walk. That meant she had less than an hour to get ready.

She assembled her outfit and placed the hangers of clothing over doorknobs.

Carefully, by pulling the elastic back before lifting, she removed her hair bonnet and tossed it atop the vanity. At this point in her life, she kept her hair short. Just enough for the natural curls to do their thing while being simple to manage.

"Alvin, your Chickie has some serious business today," she said to the room.

Her late husband thought her skin had the same shading as the chicory he liked to add to his morning coffee. Chickie had been his pet name for her throughout the forty years they'd been married.

She realized for the first time since her bathroom prayer that this task would also allow her an indulgence she'd not had since Alvin's passing. When he was alive, she liked to have one thing in her life that was only hers, private and unknown to everyone else. It lost strength once all her actions in the house were known only by her. Public ones too. Public and private all ran together in a solitary life.

Miss Melba reached for her moisturizer as a flurry of paws swept in on a wave of manic energy. A hearty meow was followed by a fierce twitch of the nose, moustache with it.

"Allen Toussaint, you are so debonair. Did you use your litter yet?"

6

Bobby Delery knew there was nothing he could do about a runaway gurney. The squad cars turned sideways would prevent it from entering the intersection.

He shook his head and turned back around to continue following the blood trail and checking for witnesses. "What the hell have I gotten myself into?" he asked.

Delery didn't come to another house either inhabited or with an answered door until midway down the block past Villere.

On the left side of the street were a nicely kept double and adjacent single, both painted a light Caribbean blue with white trim. A wooden fence connected the two. The single had no front door or window.

The instant he knocked, the door opened, as if by premonition.

"Yessir?" the man said. He looked to be in his 70's.

Delery delivered his spiel, making sure to "sir" the man back with respect.

"I ain't seen nothin' up there that far away, sure enough as my name's Rudolph Chesnutt."

Delery responded with his follow-up.

"I woke up 'round then. Had some food disagree wit' my belly. Mighta even gave me hallucinations," Chesnutt said.

"What do you mean, Mr. Chesnutt?" Delery replied, thinking the next step was to extract himself and move on.

Chesnutt leaned in as if about to impart a major secret. "I seen a ghost wit' my own eyes. Y'hear?"

"In your house?"

"Nawsir." He pointed with a callused finger. "Out there. Walkin' down the street."

Delery's attention clicked on. "Sir, what did it look like?"

The man looked away with sheepish eyes.

"Least I thought it were a ghost 'cuz the face and arms, them legs too, all so white they glowin'. These street lamps be's out, but it were walkin' real slow. Glowin' in the moonlight. A man. Now that I think of it, this were more like a conjure. Y'hear?"

"A conjure man? In what way, Mr. Chesnutt?"

"I heard its voice talkin' 'bout 'red rooster blood' like a, a, you know the words a psychic or a conjure say. Incantation talk."

"An incantation?" Delery replied.

Chesnutt nodded. "Yeah. Tha's it. Incantation. Glowin' like moonlight in the gutter. Whitest thing I ever seen. Y'hear? Talkin' like a conjure. Carryin' his sacrifice."

"Wait, what do you mean by sacrifice?" Delery quizzed.

Rudolph Chesnutt's lips puckered. "It were a big container. Yessir, the weight musta been heavy 'cuz the way the conjure walked. One foot strugglin' after the other. Y'hear me? Lotsa dead things inside, prob'ly."

Delery pushed. "Was there anything else you recall?"

"Jes that it had a big bag on its back. Like a astronaut. Like them dirty white chil'ren come in on the train. Them hobo types. Big bag."

"Anything else, sir?"

"Nawsir, well 'cept that conjure were spittin' bright red blood. Musta been rooster blood it drank."

Delery extended his hand. "Thank you for your time, Mr. Chesnutt."

"Alright, alright. Use-ta do a little detective work myself. Holla at ya later."

Bobby Delery knew he'd heard a piece of the puzzle, but it was skewed. He didn't doubt what Rudolph Chesnutt saw. The kaleidoscope image needed to be made clearer, though.

The rest of the block canvassing consisted of a threat, a

no-answer, and a woman who asked him if he wanted to come in and take off his socks.

Twenty minutes later he continued on. The blood trail continued to the left, down Urquhart. Looking across the street, Delery whispered, "That is some serious target hardening."

He was referring to the idea of crime-proofing a home or business.

"There must be something of major value on the other side of that fence to have metal girders supporting it," he continued.

In the rest of the block, a partly-ramshackle hybrid fence extended on the left. The blood trail disappeared. A pile of tires and trash were strewn on the right just before a gravel path crossed.

Delery followed the street all the way up to the train tracks, missing the blood spots on and near the fence beforehand. He looked off to the left at the overpass and saw no more first responders up there, but the blood trail continued at his feet.

"Just me now, but I'm getting closer," he said.

The blood trail was lost on the tracks, but without question he had to follow across and see what continued on the other side.

After ducking through a mangled chain link fence, the street and dried blood continued.

At Montegut, a warehouse stretched the length of the block to his right. Delery read the sign on a delivery truck parked in front. Soft Touch Linen Services.

"Here's where it is. The heart of the city's beating around this area," he said.

One of the few news stories unrelated to crime Delery had read on NOLA.com before his move was about eight little children who had died over a six month period at Crescent Hospital. All the deaths by a flesh eating fungus were eventually traced to the linens. Soft Touch washed for restaurants, hospitals, hotels, and organizations with uniforms.

There was a good possibility that negligence on the part of the hospital staff was reason for the bed linens, towels, or gowns picking up the fungus. Responsibility would soon be fought out in court.

"I'm back in a rainy humid sub-tropical place that breeds all this," he thought.

Delery knew there were other cities in the country with a similar climate, but none of them felt like New Orleans. That's partly why he was back. Chicago winters had paid a toll on him for years, so he was ready for a change of pace.

"But here I am, second day back, and they already got me working," he said.

A few colleagues had teased him with light humor, awkwardness, or befuddled ribbing.

"Delery, is your office on Bourbon Street? Don't take off too much for the beads."

"Are you gonna start saying y'all to get in practice?"

"You're from there, right? What else is there to do besides Mardi Gras?"

"Nawlins? That's the hotbed of active precipitation," not meaning rain but the controversial criminology theory that some victims bring about their own harm or death.

"Here's how you know the difference between NOPD and the gang bangers. The kids are the ones with better guns."

"I was there once. The place smells."

And then there was Shanice.

Shanice Baker was a striking adjunct sociology professor. Up in Chicago, they called her "redbone." Down in New Orleans, they'd say "Creole." Both places would use "bright." All those ways of describing a light-skinned black woman, either from respect, jealousy, or fetishizing.

She had an active mind, an outgoing smile, and a full head

of natural hair. Curly and pulled back from her face.

Shanice and Delery dated on and off, but other than in the bedroom, they just didn't have that certain something that two people fall into and continue to grow from if they're meant to be together. Actually, she felt it, but he didn't.

All this made Delery feel low about himself. If it didn't click in his heart with a woman like Shanice, chances for the future weren't good.

He was in his early 40's and had never married. For years, he was content to play the field but was feeling a pull to settle down. Shanice seemed like the perfect woman, but without love he couldn't do it.

Delery told Shanice his secret when they got close. He typically didn't reveal it to the women he dated, intelligent beauties across the spectrum of class and race, though most of his girlfriends over the years had been black. He'd made the mistake of revealing his secret once, years before, to a bank manager who promptly hopped her pasty little ass right out of bed.

He knew Shanice was good with a secret, though. She'd had a similar fish-out-of-water experience growing up in Arizona. They grew to be solid friends, occasionally erotic friends when the need struck.

When he was packing up his office, she stopped in. "Bobby, I know you feel like a man without a home. You're crying out inside. Saying, 'This is who I am.' I truly wish you the best. Do you. I hope you find your place."

She leaned in. "Don't worry about me spreading talk when you're gone. Hope I see you again, baby."

Delery knew he'd miss terribly their walks in Grant Park, record digging around town, and so much more, but that couldn't keep him from doing what he needed to do. He hoped New Orleans held the answer.

This all looped through his mind while he stood leaned over and staring at dried blood near the Urquhart and Feliciana intersection. Delery looked too at his shirt and pants, realizing that the heat and humidity had taken care of his wrinkled clothing.

After speaking with the young white guys on the right who operated an underground pizza joint and the older black couple on the left who ran two food trucks, it sounded like the ghost/conjure man/dripper-of-blood had walked through talking the same talk about a red rooster. There was also a fist-sized red mark almost four feet up on one of the food trucks that looked like more blood.

The trail ended, though, before the Clouet intersection.

"Did he go inside or did it just dry up?" Delery asked himself.

There was no answer at the first house on the left on Clouet. He suspected the hand-written sign taped inside the screen door reading "Frozen Cups – Pink, Lemonade, Green Apple, Grape - $.25; Giant Freeze - $2" likely meant the inhabitant was an elderly lady who either didn't hear him knock or was already at church.

A boarded up school filled the entire block on the opposite side. Delery figured the character he was after couldn't have scaled the fence and barbed wire surrounding the perimeter.

It was like Red Rooster, as Delery started thinking of him, had up and disappeared.

He was about to turn back and continue downriver on Urquhart when he saw something that stirred him up.

"That is the whitest white man I've ever seen. The color of paper," Delery couldn't help but say aloud. A tall slightly hunched guy was slowly making his way down the sidewalk along the school. The sun's reflection hit his skin and caused Delery to shield his eyes.

It was like a pale solar flare. "This must be the glowing man

Mr. Chesnutt was talking about. Red Rooster."

Delery peeked through his fingers. He was able to make out a moustache that resembled a mop before the dirty water had been wrung out, a dark t-shirt and tan splotchy shorts, as well as what appeared to be a backpack.

Still shielding his eyes as he strode from the sidewalk to the street, Delery knew this was his big break. The two were right across from each other, getting closer by the second, when the other man realized Delery was heading for him.

Just then, a tan van painted New Life Baptist Church on the side sped up the street, pulled between them, and idled. Its large bold letters left no room for inclusion of street address. Delery was unable to see in because of its tinted windows.

The church van stopped only briefly. Delery waited in place for it to pass.

When it did, he took a step toward the man, but the linen-white figure really had disappeared this time. "Shit! You've got to be kidding me," Delery said.

The van was already to Villere, so there was no chance of running after it.

Delery didn't know where the church was located. He had Commander Jones' number, though.

"Sir, this is Bobby Delery, out in the vicinity of the crime scene," Delery announced, back at the sidewalk.

"Delery, you find anything?"

"I think so. I almost had contact with a person of interest who got away. Can you get a squad car over to New Life Baptist Church?"

"New Life Baptist Church?" Jones questioned.

"The man hopped into their van. I couldn't catch it."

Delery described the glowing man and what prior information led to his identification, leaving out a few details.

"You're not putting me on?"

"No sir. Saw him myself," Delery said.

"Okay. I'll send some uniforms over there. A chalky white man in an African-American church shouldn't be too tricky to spot."

"Thank you, sir," Delery said, relieved that he wasn't getting the brush-off like from Captain Connell.

"No. Thank you. Continue on. Can you get over to the Quarter by midday? Club Big Easy on Bourbon Street, between St. Louis and Toulouse. You want to speak with Dom Cavallari. He's the one who runs the place. Don't go in like a cowboy."

"Got it."

Jones paused. "And Delery, remember why I asked you out there. Cavallari's the only one you talk to. See if you can pick up something my guys missed."

"Will do, sir."

"Remember, we've got to act fast, but again, kid gloves at the club."

After concluding formalities, Delery decided to head back to his car.

A red Toyota Corolla came booming up the street. It was stolen in a Mid City carjacking a week prior. The guns inside were also stolen. Blue Shoes' .45 was from a Jefferson Parish gun owner who didn't lock his car doors. Stink's .38 came from an Uptown robbery. Neither firearm was used solely for protection.

"I might could hit a lick," Blue Shoes said from the driver's side.

"Naw, naw. " Stink replied.

"You jes wanna smash Lyric," Blues Shoes accused.

Stink admitted, matter of fact, "Fuck yeah. I wanna smash her alla time. She got impossible moves. Lyric always take me right up to the mountaintop."

"Shit, nigga. They all do. You gonna wife that bitch."

"Naw, you crazy. Ain't gonna wife nobody." Stink firmed up. "Lookit. Where he think he is? This Clouet Kinfolk streets."

They pulled up next to Bobby Delery who was walking on the sidewalk and about to turn on Urquhart, heading toward the train yard.

"Hey! Gotta light?" Blue Shoes called out.

Delery knew what this was about. The day wasn't going his way. "Quick reply and run around the corner. They probably won't back up to come after me," he thought.

He didn't have a chance to act, though. Blues Shoes had him looking down the barrel of a gun.

"Bag, muthafucka. Phone too."

Delery paused, frozen. He'd only had a gun pointed at him twice before.

"C'mon, bitch. Ain't got all day. Don't make me get out this car."

With heavy cautious steps, Delery walked up to the car. He leaned down and removed his shoulder bag.

The robbery was disrupted by a squad car barreling up Clouet. Blue Shoes shoved Delery away from the car with his free hand. Delery was in an awkward stance, and he fell to the ground backward. The Corolla flew off.

Delery was breathing heavily and loudly. "At least I'm safe now," he whispered between gasps.

A swirl of heat, car doors, and yelling proved otherwise.

He was roughly rolled onto his stomach and searched.

"You selling drugs?" "Keep your fucking hands there;" "Don't move, faggot;" "Who you dealing for?" were a few of the flurry of commands and accusations thrown out.

"Officers, I'm a criminologist helping NOPD," he tried, attempting to see them better through the sun's glare. He couldn't make out faces or badge numbers.

"I'm looking at a driver's license that tells me you're a goddamn liar. Illinois. So, you dealing or buying?" was asked in an accent from the sticks.

The other cop answered his partner. "He's acting like he's on drugs. Breathing heavy. Sweating."

Delery tried again. "Officers, I'm breathing erratically because I almost got robbed. I'm sweaty because it's summer in New Orleans. I'm…"

"Shut the fuck up, bitch!" A shoe ground his head into the grass.

"His bag's clean." Delery's utility knife wasn't found in its tucked away spot in the bag.

"You dumb motherfucking idiots come down here, show no common sense, and expect us to protect you," the cop with the foot said, pushing hard once again before stepping off Delery.

"Come on," his partner, the hick, said. "Let's get over to that Baptist church and see if we can find the white guy there. Of all the places to hide out."

Delery pulled himself off the ground. "I'm the one who saw that guy and called Commander Jones. Hurry, get to the church."

His words only hit the backs of the two officers and fell to the street next to his discarded shoulder bag. They drove off and he sat on the ground, cleaning off his clothes that were wrinkled again.

7

Hutch woke himself up with a flurry of deep coughing. For a flash he forgot where he was, but it all quickly came back to him.

He was covered in sweat. Sore left knee. Back in knots from sleeping on the floor. Pieces of debris matted to his skin and clothing. He stunk.

He sat up, looked around, and shook his head.

His hide-out space was decently lit, considering, and it looked worse by day. The holes in the roof and front windows allowed the sharp sun to cast slivers of light across the mess. The multiple angles of sun rays made Hutch think of search lights or as if he were the focus of a magnifying glass.

He saw a calendar still turned to August 2005 curling up on the wall, along with newspaper clippings and hand-written thoughts about Turner's Soul Food restaurants being run by white supremacists to poison black people. The previous tenant was trying to prove the rumor was true.

If he were prone to tears, they would've flowed, but Hutch wasn't one for crying. Instead, he croaked out, "Alright. Stay strong."

He stood up, winced, and looked outside the window. Not much activity on the street. Only a steady flow of cars. One of them announced itself in advance with a booming radio.

"It's 10:25. Gonna be a hot day here in the Crescent City," the radio announcer said.

He sat back down slowly. "Man, what were you thinkin'?" he wondered. "I done fucked up."

Oddly, no rats or mice had been heard, not even cockroaches, but Hutch knew they were around. He hated the idea of speaking to them, so he worked through it all in his mind rather than aloud.

He'd gotten a jeep with solid VIN, license plate, and registration. Nothing stolen, so it wouldn't be obvious if the cops scanned the plate or pulled them over.

Driver's licenses and a passport for him were even easier to obtain, though more expensive. Hutch knew of Tommy J's operation out of an abandoned Harvey strip mall space. Hutch's was a Texas license. Olson's was a California one. They'd both been given new names. Paul Grayson for Olson and Maurice Richard for Hutch.

He'd knocked at the door, said the password "Kenyatta," and entered the former Walgreens. Covered windows belied the action going on inside. Over twenty underage kids sat waiting until their number was called. They were all there for fake ID's.

The operation was run like a mini-DMV. Two computers were hooked up to two stolen driver's license printers and laminators. Hutch had been in the week prior since the passport was more expensive and took longer. Like then, Hutch didn't take a number but walked directly over to the head man.

Tommy J did good clean work. With the passport too. Hutch had passed on the credit card skimmers and the guns offered but examined the fake documents carefully.

"I ain't need no hammer," he'd told Tommy J. "I got some methodical shit, don't require no fire."

The other man, wiry and with intense eyes, peered through his glasses and beard, shrugging.

"Alright, Hutch. Man always need a hammer, but you keep on. This some good craftsmanship here."

Hutch grunted in agreement. "I 'ppreciate that."

"I 'ppreciate you 'ppreciatin', but I need second half-a my fee," Tommy J said seriously.

"I'm good for it. Don't stress. $2,800, right?" Hutch asked

and flipped the band off the folded roll from his front pocket before counting it out.

"Yeah. $28 front end. $28 back. I'm too blessed to be stressed, baby. 5K a good price for that passport. Ain't stolen from no tourist."

"We see how she work. Thank you, brother," Hutch said.

Birdsong on the roof refocused Hutch on the present.

"Damn. $5,600 for the passport and licenses. Olson paid his $300. All that shit for the jeep. I cleared my bank account. Sold off a bunch-a shit. Didn't pay rent for two months. Twelve big bills and some pocket change all I got in this world. That cruise to Brazil leaving in six hours," he thought.

He considered, "All's I gotta do, get over by I-10 going west and hitch a ride. Plenty semi's out there. I'm good once I'm on the highway."

Hutch laughed a grim laugh, remembering, "Course I could get a cab to Houston, but I can't burn off too much this money." Like everyone, he'd heard about or knew desperate people paying cabbies to evacuate them both before and after the flood.

He coughed again and quickly covered his mouth so he couldn't be heard outside. Who knew how many people were out looking for him?

"It was goin' just right," he thought, "but not for too long."

Hutch remembered Club Big Easy having a good night. Packed house. He'd discreetly observed Mr. C sending off his two henchmen before going into a certain weekly routine. It took a little time for the manager to finally walk to the back, accompanied.

Waiting seemed interminable. To ease the tension, he'd made a loop around the room. Dave, the other bouncer, had questioned him.

"Hutch, what's up? It's all good here. You all right, bruh?"

The older man played with him a bit to take the pressure off. Plus, he knew Dave would be questioned later, so decoy statements were vital. It was one of those stories that black people would love to tell gullible white people, both for their own enjoyment and to know that at some point later white folks would be gathering around hearing it retold, all saying, "Those people are crazy."

Hutch rarely had a chance to do this. How often did white men, much less women, express concern for him or take focus off of themselves? So, he spun a yarn about baby mamas in Slidell and Plaquemines; money owed to men in Algiers and Belle Chasse; dice games in Hollygrove; a night of drinking in a bar on Elysian Fields that ended in a shootout; and more. By the time he got to the end, Dave's mouth was slack and eyes were buggy.

Hutch couldn't resist. "Brer Soul's got a life, don't he?" He kept from an overt smile. It was the first time he saw a white man get ashy.

Now that the edge was off, he turned around to see Clint Olson descending the stairs with a large beer case.

Hutch eyeballed the back. No sign of Mr. C.

Olson walked steadily to the front door. Like Hutch planned, Olson said, loudly enough for Dave and the shot girl Bree to hear, "Hey Hutch. Mr. C wants this in his trunk. You walk with? Watch my back so no knuckleheads jump me?"

Dave was dazed and Bree was new. Neither blinked an eye when Hutch played his part perfectly. "You can't handle that shit yourself? Alright, c'mon. Be back in a minute, Dave."

The dark blue jeep was parked on Dauphine near St. Peter. It contained no suitcases, only a full tank of gas. No rain was in the forecast, so Hutch hadn't bothered to purchase a canvas top.

Hutch and Olson stepped out of the club together.

Under his breath, Hutch said, "Not a word 'til we cross the street."

A circle of tourists were gathered around three black high energy acrobatic dancers who were performing on a colorful drop cloth to music from two speakers as powerful as those inside the clubs. That part of Bourbon was slightly wider than the rest and allowed a rounder arc.

The dancer wearing a wireless microphone paused and announced to the crowd, "You might wonder how we got so good at our moves. Five words. Running…from…the…po-lice."

At this the mostly white crowd belly laughed. A few threw dollar bills into the middle.

Hutch had heard this line and its predictable response several times over the years, and it never failed to make him feel darker than blue. He told Olson to follow him and roughly pushed through the crowd into the dancer's space.

Looking at the dancers with fierce eyes, Hutch said, "I'm happy not to see your raggedy Uncle Tommin' asses no more. Fuckin' bitch ass niggers." He could take all three of them on and they knew it, so they all turned away, cleaning imaginary specks of dirt on their sweat pants. Hutch didn't need to push through the other side of the crowd since they quickly opened up space for him, with Olson following behind. They were steps from Toulouse.

"You got it?" Hutch asked.

"Yeah, yeah. I can't believe it," Olson replied.

"Keep walkin'. Box full?"

"Yeah, totally full. I can't believe how easy it was."

At the intersection, Hutch took a long look down Bourbon both ways. All was well. Not so when he checked down Toulouse toward the river.

He and Olson were in the midst of other people, but they

were spotted by Johnny and Big T, midway in the block, still making the rounds for weekly pick-ups. Hutch's response was suspicious and he knew it. He saw them register surprise. He also knew the jeep was almost two blocks away.

Olson was initially angry when Hutch grabbed the beer case from him, but then he saw the urgency of the older man's eyes.

"Mr. C's men. They saw us," sputtered Hutch.

Their pace quickened significantly, though they couldn't full-on run due to the weight of money, even with Hutch carrying it.

They took the sidewalk on the right, lucky that Johnny and Big T were also weighed down by money that couldn't be discarded. The two Sicilians had less weight to carry, though, so they were making up ground.

Five observant streetcorner hustlers saw the chased and chasers, sussed out at a glance who to help, and meandered into the intersection. Johnny and Big T were awkwardly walk-jogging down the middle of the street at this point.

"Get the fuck outta the way," the two barked, unable to use their hands to clear a way through the cluster.

"'Scuse;" "Oh, yes sir;" "Who you think you talkin' to?" "Sorry, mister;" and "Lookit them sad shoes;" were the too-casual replies. As soon as the Sicilians passed, the common good also passed, and the five men went back to giving each other the evil eye.

By this time, Hutch and Olson were at Dauphine. They veered off to the right and stayed in the street.

Hutch was bent forward at the waist, both arms around the money, focused ahead with determination. No more looking back.

Olson's eyes were filled with fear. He was moving his arms like many untrained joggers. Flailing sideways like a frightened chicken. No efficiency of motion.

"What the fuck you doin'?" Hutch asked through deep breaths.

Olson whimpered back. "What do you mean? I'm running for my life."

"Get them arms down. You pop me with that elbow, I'm leavin' you for the Eye-talians."

"Okay. I'm sorry. I'm really sorry," Olson replied subserviently, meaning not only his lack of form but also the whole scam to get the skims. He continued running the same way.

They didn't know it, but Big T was the only one behind them. Johnny had continued up Toulouse to Burgundy to retrieve his Ford Explorer.

Midway in the block from Hutch and Olson, a group of eight men in their early 30's loudly commandeered the street. They were in the French Quarter for all night drinking and dancing. Five were wearing polo shirts of various types, all tucked in sensible slacks. They had hoped to conquer women at the Gold Mine Saloon but were reduced to walking like two-year-olds. They were drunk. They were a short drive to home. They were from Metairie.

"How many…tell me…how many Flaming Dr. Pepper's I drank?" one of them slurred to the others, who had formed a loose line across Dauphine.

Hutch and Olson were about five car lengths away from them.

"Comin' through. Make room," Hutch urged.

Olson nodded vigorously, his flailing hands still up in the 10 and 2 driving position, his elbows remaining in their sideways angle.

The suburbanites paid no attention to this, thinking if at all, that the jogging men would yield before reaching them.

Hutch called out again, louder. "Get the fuck out the way!"

Two car lengths now.

Olson, at his right, started to ask, "What are we…," but saw in his peripheral vision that Hutch was lowering his head to prepare himself. In his own way, Olson did the same. With his dropped head and raised swinging arms, he was a sight.

At one car length, the group got frightened and attempted to move but stumbled into each other.

Hutch turned wide shoulders slightly to his left in preparation. The jeep was steps away.

At impact, he dropped his head so that the crown was facing straight ahead like a battering ram. Then in quick motion he lifted it. "Uhhhh!" he snarled.

Hutch sent two of the men airborne into a beige BMW whose alarm promptly screamed through the night. He hit them so hard it would've stripped white from rice.

Olson, on the other hand, was so top heavy by his stance that he went into and over one of the men before performing a series of misshapen somersaults. His high arms served to protect his head.

A voice from across the street called out, "Look at that muthafucka roll."

Hutch regained open field and was to the jeep in seconds. He looked back while pulling the keys from his pocket to see Olson spinning down the street, a bewildered group of drunkards, and Big T gaining ground.

Hutch opened the door, set the beer case on the passenger floor, and stepped back out to stop Olson and pull him to his feet.

"C'mon, Clint," Hutch ordered.

Meanwhile, a big white SUV was screeching as it turned from Burgundy against the one-way street St. Peter. A cab was in its way, so the Ford Explorer veered off to the right, drove up on the sidewalk, and sped past. A man wearing a beret and a leather vest stepped out of the Gold Mine and shook his head.

Hutch and Olson quickly got into the jeep. The second Hutch started it and prepared to pull out of the parking spot, he began honking to clear the khaki hoard from the street.

This time they listened. Big T planted himself in the path of the jeep, but as he saw it careening at him, he dove out of the way, still holding onto the bags of skims he'd picked up earlier.

Hutch hit the gas even harder. He had them to Canal in a matter of seconds. By this time, Johnny had picked up Big T. The SUV was barely a block away.

Hutch's plan had been that they'd cross Canal, get on I-10 going west, and take it all the way to Houston. At Canal, though, they had a red light and too much traffic in the left and middle lanes, so he tore around the corner to the right.

He wanted to get over but was stuck in the right lane. He ran the lights at Rampart, Basin, Treme, and Marais. Cross traffic was light, so there were no problems. A young security guard in a beat-up Honda Civic was looking down, texting his girlfriend that he was on the way home, so he didn't see how close he was to a collision.

The light at Claiborne was green, and Hutch made a quick right, hoping to throw the Sicilians off, but it didn't work.

"I'm gonna get away from 'em. Belt up," Hutch said. Olson ignored him but whined, "I'll never get to San Diego."

Hutch knew the cross streets by the cemetery rarely got traffic, so he chose those blocks to click his own seatbelt in place. The SUV stayed firmly on their heels, not trying to pass, merely following.

Hutch was dreading the next light. Night life was hopping on Orleans. There were good-timers, high-rollers, and wanna-be's dotting that stretch, in and outside the clubs.

He started honking in advance. The light turned in his favor, but a man was walking with a woman across Claiborne. He was old, tall, and skinny, with a fresh high and tight trim, leaving only hair on the top of his head. She was young, thick-bodied, and had long braids. They were both high and ready for each other's action. Like all good New Orleanians, they didn't look up at the source of the honking, figuring it could just go around them.

Hutch kept blasting away.

Tall and skinny was trying to seduce. "I ain't gonna lie. Matta fact I think you…Oh my!"

He saw the jeep bearing down on them and pulled her forward with him in a big jump. Hutch swerved past them. She tottered on her heels and went down sitting. Her light long summer dress typically extended to her toes, but as she fell, the slits on each side worked like a parachute, and flew up to her hips.

The eyes of tall and skinny, still standing, bugged out.

She cursed and swung her purse at him, and its contents emptied to the street, many of which were promptly run over by the passing white SUV. She tried to get up, slipped and fell down again, scooted on her rear, and angrily pulled tall and skinny down to the pavement with her. He tried to shield himself from her slapping.

The crowd outside Jo-Ro's Lounge erupted in laughter. Eyes emptied with tears. Men fell to the ground holding their sides. Women slid down to the sidewalk smacking their own legs. Catcalls abounded.

"That juicy tail ain't never leaving the street," one of them called out.

"Get him, girl," another said.

"You gonna get it for half price now, Harold!" shouted a smart ass, which sent another wave of people falling down to the sidewalk.

Hutch and Olson were holding a gambler's lucky hand at the street lights. They hit Esplanade and St. Bernard, both busy intersections, at greens and sped through untouched.

Just past Elysian Fields, Claiborne going downriver turned into Robertson. Hutch zigged and zagged a bit around traffic at the Elysian Fields dual lights, blew through both at St. Roch, and had a green for both at Franklin. The SUV, though, did the same.

A deep cough rumbled Hutch to his waist. The recent memory of a plan dissolved in the moldy soup of the present.

"Right now I should be sleepin' in Houston, dreamin' 'bout drivin' to Galveston and takin' a cruise to Brazil," he whispered, shaking his head.

The plan was that Olson would drop him off at the cruise ship terminal where Hutch's trip was already booked under the name Maurice Richard. Olson would drive alone to his new place. The money would all be divided up before then.

Hutch had decided when the cruise ship arrived at port in Salvador, Brazil, he'd disembark normally with everyone else but melt into the city and make it his home.

"Stay strong. Can still get there. Gotta mission to change my condition," he murmured, standing up again to look through the window.

8

Two Russians faced two Sicilians. There was open hostility on each side of the hallway. All of them had the physiques of NFL linemen who were no longer in shape.

The Sicilian duo was hostile because they were unarmed. Their pieces were removed from the shoulder holsters and taken at the front door earlier. The Russian duo was hostile because they *were* armed.

Excessive steroid use had thinned the hair of each man. The gel they all used made each of their heads look like the product of a hasty artist. Simple blocky skulls with a few swept back hairs as if afterthoughts.

They were standing outside a closed door. The décor throughout the house could only be described as ostentatious. The structure itself resembled those surrounding it along a tony section of Lakeview. Six pillars in front, though, left only comparisons to a well-moneyed frat house.

The four men were on the job. None of them could emit a minute of charm anyway. Wasn't what they were hired for. The air around them was one giant pregnant pause whose water was about to break.

The determiner of "if" and "when" was on the other side of the door. His name was Alex Yevchev. He spoke English with a Northern Russian accent. Yevchev dressed and adorned himself with jewelry of the type that newly wealthy young men are given to. Skin was cadaverous. His expression, however, was very much alive.

To say he was angry would be an understatement. For the time being, it was wrapped in the veneer of a steely falcon waiting out its dinner.

"Dominic, you are not following me. I do not get fucked. I do the fucking."

"Mr. Yevchev, I'm telling you. I don't know how they got the combination. I didn't write it down. I told nobody. Just your mouth to my ears. I know it looks bad they got the safe open. But they did." Dominic Cavallari, known as Mr. C to his employees, was in the hot seat.

"Do you think I am stupid?"

"No, not at all."

"I am trying to understand how the safe in your office is emptied of my money. I am also trying to understand how you do not know when it is happening."

Cavallari was struggling. "There was a disturbance downstairs. I needed to deal with it."

Yevchev's teeth shone like they were ready for prey. "Do you not have bouncers for that?" he asked, reeling in the other, at least thirty years senior to his age of twenty-eight.

"Yes, but this was a vio…a disturbance that was a little worse than usual," Cavallari said, trying not to use the word "violent" or anything like it.

"You are downstairs and your bouncer, this monkey you call Hutch, is not in his place? And your two men, the fools outside my door, are nowhere to be found?"

"Mr. Yevchev, they were out doing pick-ups. The other clubs. The escort places. All the rest. It takes a little time." Cavallari tried to re-focus the subject.

Yevchev couldn't be swayed.

"Do *you* think I do not know where my money comes from? You are not thinking with your head."

"No, no. I wasn't implying…"

"Shut up. Shut your fucking mouth. You say many things to me like I am a stupid man to you. But you, you are the one not thinking with a head."

Cavallari was confused by this. He expected full-on ferocity. That's what he trucked in himself. What he knew. He couldn't follow indirection.

"Huh? What do you mean?"

"What do I mean?" Yevchev's left hand had been picking at his goatee or impatiently tapping on a bottle throughout the encounter, but now he raised his claw and pointed it across the desk. The diamond bevel in his large watch seemed to pulse.

"I mean you are thinking with your prick." He circled his pinky finger. "With your tiny Sicilian prick," he accused.

Cavallari felt his head clamped. He briefly closed his eyes and winced.

"There is only one reason you are still alive. It is your tiny prick."

Yevchev continued.

"I will now tell you a thing. When it was the time that my people, strong Russian people of the earth, make the deal with your people, old tired Sicilians, for a piece of the action, we still do not trust you. A Sicilian would piss on his own mother and cut her throat for a little money. We do not trust you. We installed our own cameras in our clubs, okay? From the *beginning*."

The vise around Cavallari's head cranked tighter. Beads of sweat appeared on his forehead. He'd already soaked through his undershirt.

"We keep you on because your people vouch for you. They call you 'loyal.' They call you 'no nonsense.' This sounds good to my people. We do not have to bring in new guys and set it up. It is already set up. This is good for us. Yet, we do not trust you."

Yevchev's eyes narrowed.

"What do you do with people you do not trust? You check on them. Watch carefully. What they do. For three years we watch you with our cameras. I have been pleased with what I have seen except for one thing. Do you know what that is, Dominic? The flaw?"

Cavallari's ears were popping from the build-up of pressure. Yevchev wasn't expecting a reply.

"*This* is what I have seen week after week. I have seen you on the first floor away from the office at the same time every weekend your two men are doing their pick-ups. I have seen you look around the room. You spend time doing this. Making your choice. I have seen you speak to the bartender. I have seen the bartender nod at you. Do you see where I am going, Dominic?"

Cavallari began shaking; his knees, his hands on his knees, and his feet. Yevchev kept on.

"Here is where. From our cameras, I have seen the bartender put a pill in a drink and give it to a shot girl. She takes it to someone, the one who is your choice, for free. He is different every week but always looks the same. Most of the time he accepts the free drink, and the girl goes off to sell her test tube shots. Yes, he always looks the same. He is young and his I.D. did not get checked at the door. He is with one friend. Maybe two. No more. He is pretty. What do I see next? I have seen you wait before discreetly directing him away from his friends. Through the dance floor and into the courtyard. Yes, Dominic. You leave my money in my safe with no protection because you are thinking with your tiny fucking prick."

Yevchev began to thunder. Tension also increased among the four outside the room.

"So, what do we do, Dominic? We put another camera in the little room where you take your pretty boys. I cannot watch this shit you do, so I make my guys watch it. Kostya and Pavel on the other side of the door. What do they tell me? I hear that you have a little prick and are a bad man."

Cavallari's inner organs were wrapping around themselves.

"We keep these videos, Dominic, so you cannot fuck us like your little boys. You are not in the ground right now only because we have video from early this morning. We have seen your second floor bartender enter your office, open my safe, and put my money in a big box for beer. We have seen your nigger bouncer look out for him. Both of them leave my club together. We see this. How do I first hear about my own club being robbed? Not from you. On the computer. Because you yell and make noise about it that is overheard by a reporter."

Yevchev paused and threw back a drink. He cleared his throat after having a second one.

"There are things I know. You did not help Clint Olson open the safe, but he opened it easily. He is now dead. Many stories are in the news by mosquito reporters about my club. They do not say my name. It will stay that way. Yes? It is time to find out things I do not know. How the bartender opened my safe. How we will find Hutch and my money. It is time for your fools to come in."

Cavallari tried to speak. "Mr. Yevchev, you don't…"

"Shut up. A man who cannot be trusted will only speak the truth by one method. It is how I find out the space between what you say and what you do." He called out, "Kostya! Pavel! Bring them."

Johnny and Big T were already suffering from sore necks and backs after driving into a house a few hours earlier. Lack of sleep and a bad feeling heightened the aching.

The larger of the two Russians grunted across the hall and gestured to the others. All four rose together, the one called Kostya opened the door, and the Russians waited to follow the Sicilians inside.

Johnny and Big T entered with heavy steps, stopping a few feet behind the chair Cavallari was seated in with his back to them. They felt an exceptionally menacing presence in the room. The air conditioning was blasting and the shadows of Cavallari's lies were cast around the room. Kostya and Pavel fanned off slightly so they could see Yevchev while maintaining firm control over the two in front of them.

Yevchev spoke as a gracious host. "Dominic, your men have been waiting. They must be thirsty." He held up a sleek bottle with the bust of a man in profile pictured toward the top.

Johnny and Big T replied with polite nervous denials in unison.

"I see you have manners, but please. I am offering. You must accept," Yevchev soothed.

Johnny and Big T fell over each other with their excessively formal refusals. These were men who picked their noses and scratched their crotches in public, so manners hung on them like fine drapes in a zoo.

"Hmmm. Maybe you think vodka is only a drink for Russians? That it will not sit well on your Sicilian tongues? It is wrong, this thought. I do not drink vodka because I am a strong Russian."

At this, Kostya and Pavel subtly turned their heads toward each other.

"No, no. Let me explain, so you can understand," Yevchev said. He set the bottle down and pointed at it.

"This is Chopin Vodka. It is made in Poland, a country of farmers. This man pictured is Chopin."

Yevchev mused.

"He was a famous musician from this same place. They are honoring their countryman. I do not know a fucking thing about Chopin, but that does not matter. This vodka from Poland is made of potatoes. It is the best. I am from Kirov Oblast. Potatoes are in my blood. My people have bled for potatoes. Many years ago. You must not deny my request.

Please, which of you will drink first?"

To strengthen the gesture, Yevchev poured three fingers worth into a cut crystal glass next to his own.

Big T shrugged and stepped forward to accept. Pavel, who was behind him, pulled out a gun doubled in length by a long cylindrical silencer and watched intently. Both he and Konstantin, known as Kostya, exchanged firm glances.

Yevchev handed the glass to Big T, who threw it back and nodded in appreciation. There was no toast. Big T started to walk back to his spot but stumbled slightly on the edge of an expensive Persian rug when he saw Pavel's gun. He regained himself and squared his shoulders, especially so, when Yevchev ordered, "Turn around."

The Russian was now standing behind his desk, screwing his own silencer in place. He did this patiently and methodically. Yevchev breathed in and out loudly through his nostrils, stared at Cavallari, and finally let his thoughts take wing.

"You are the one with the flaw, Dominic, but you are worth more to me alive."

"Mr. Yevchev, we'll find the money, my men and I," Cavallari assured.

As if he'd heard nothing, Yevchev said, "It is a sad thing if the one responsible for the loss of my money is not held accountable. The fucking monkey Hutch is out there and must be found, but I cannot shoot you, Dominic. You will find my money. Your death would not look good now that you have brought attention to my business. How? By thinking with your prick."

Yevchev looked up in thought.

"Before you all arrived here, I had a question to understand. Who is the sacrifice for Dominic? Why should it be the one who is not afraid to step forward and drink from me? The other, the rude coward, is the sacrifice."

Johnny took a deep breath and closed his eyes.

"But then I thought, 'Sasha, these are Sicilians. They are all rude. They are all cowards. The sacrifice *for* Dominic is the one who is *like* Dominic.' I saw that clearly. The one who bends to pressure, who does not think with his head, who is ruled by his appetite, that one will accept the drink."

Johnny opened his eyes. Big T's mouth dropped.

"After my money is found, Dominic, I will chop off your tiny fucking prick. Even then, you are worth more to me alive. For now, though, I do not need you in a hospital."

Cavallari was both horrified and relieved. He moved his legs together in an unconscious shift of protection.

"Do you know what this means that I cannot chop it off right now and feed it to you? Instead, the one who accepted the drink is your sacrifice," Yevchev said.

With that, Yevchev and Pavel lit up Big T so that his large frame bounced around in a death dance. From the front. From the back. They both cleared out their magazines. Kostya took his own gun out for security, but Cavallari and Johnny didn't budge.

Yevchev delivered an unholy benediction to Big T, prone on the floor, while the Sicilians pled their own private desperation.

"Fucking piece of shit. You are nothing to me," the Russian seethed.

To Cavallari: "Two of my rugs are ruined. That is coming out of your pay. See, capitalism is a good thing."

To Johnny: "You will help this pervert return my money or the next blood is yours. Yes?"

Both men nodded the nod of assent that comes easily when you can feel a dead man's warm blood on your own skin.

Yevchev sighed.

"I am again trying to understand. *This time* you will speak the truth. First, how will you find my money?"

"We've got a bunch of NOPD officers working for us. Muckety-mucks too. Captains. Lieutenants. Hutch won't get far," Cavallari said in a shaken way. He could no longer feel his body around him.

"You will call me from the club and give me the tax information for your bouncer. My people can track his credit cards and his phone. Have you been to his house?"

"Yeah, but nobody at his place. Maybe a few leads. Nothing solid. Realize, my guys, uh, guy, almost had him."

"'Almost' is the talk of losers. I have all my money or none of it. I will not get fucked, Dominic. You see this guy, this muscle man."

Yevchev pointed at Johnny.

"He is the one to make a fist and punch. Or his foot to kick. He needs his fingers and his toes. It is only morning now. The time will come to use them."

The Russian's index finger moved to his left.

"You, Dominic, are different. You can do your job, run my business, and find my money while fingers or toes are broken. This is the question to ask yourself: 'How did my bartender open a safe easily?' Think carefully of this before you tell me. The pinky is best to start with. You are right handed, yes?"

9

Bobby Delery trudged back across the train tracks.

He was shaken up. While in Chicago, he'd pictured a far different life in New Orleans, definitely a far different arrival.

It was about to get worse.

As he was walking on St. Ferdinand back to the overpass where it all began, he saw cars up above driving across and heard lots of honking. He was tired and worn down, so his initial thoughts were anchored by fatigue and frustration. It wasn't until the next thought flashed through his mind that he started running.

Delery took the quickest way to the foot of the incline, under the overpass and along the parallel surface road. Up ahead was his car, parked where he left it, blocking the left lane. No NOPD or other vehicles were alongside anymore, and the lanes had been reopened. Cars were flying past and a tow truck was in the process of backing up to his bumper.

He yelled in advance, "That's my car!" and got to it as the tow truck driver stomped back to begin hauling it away.

"Man, what you thinkin?" the driver asked with disgust. "Can't park here. People got to get through."

"I know this looks bad, but I've been helping NOPD solve a case. They were all across here a little bit ago," Delery said. He wasn't sure what the law was in New Orleans, if his car could still be towed if he arrived in time.

The driver shook his head. "For real?"

Delery nodded. Cars were honking and immediately zipping past his car into the left lane too close for comfort.

"Shit. If that's how they do you, then *you* the one need help from the po-lice."

"I'm beginning to think you're right," Delery admitted.

"You know how this work, right? Once I got you up on my truck, you gotta pay to get your car back, even if I'm still parked right here. Your car ain't have to end up in no impound lot for them to fuck you over. Couple minutes, you woulda been stuck. $193 to get it down, my man."

"Motherfuckers. $193? They can't just call it $200," Delery burned.

"You got that right. This city sure will nickel and dime you. Listen, this just my job, alright. You still got your car. You good."

They shook hands.

Delery got in his car. No time to collect himself here.

"I didn't want to go there like this, but that's how it's got to be," he said.

Rather than taking the overpass, he turned sharply to the left and used the side access road as a U-turn back to Franklin. He made a right at the intersection, and after a few blocks, made another on Galvez. There was more blight than he remembered, but the area seemed about the same, all in all.

He kept his eyes on the left once he got near Alvar.

"It's still there, big as I remember," he said, looking at his old school, William Frantz Elementary.

When he got closer, he saw there was a sign in front with a name he didn't know. "Akili, that's odd," he said. Delery was unaware of a threatened closure before the flood and the events after, remediation from damage and charter schools entering the city.

His memory was instead threaded with his walk as a kid. Four blocks on the nose. Mama walked him there. A few kids had picked on him, but that was so far in the past. Mama told him they didn't understand, to ignore them when they said, "You don't belong here, white boy."

"She told me about the importance of this place," he said to himself.

He was taught in school that Frantz was the first one integrated in New Orleans, about a six year old black girl named Ruby Bridges getting escorted by federal marshals. Mama told him about authors like John Steinbeck coming to town to write about it, about the painting by Norman Rockwell showing Ruby, and that the Bridges family lived only a few blocks away on Johnson. "The city would've changed the school name, Bobby," she said, "but you keep the name if there's history. They only change the name if they want to forget the history."

The next few blocks were different than anything else he'd seen so far. Most houses seemed inhabited, certainly, but there were also several empty lots with overgrown weeds. A couple newly built houses too, made to look historic.

Delery wondered if flooding in this area had come from the breached Florida Avenue Canal or the Industrial Canal. The first was an open one for pumping out water. The second a shipping canal connecting the Mississippi River to Lake Pontchartrain.

As he drove along, he saw people walking or driving, going about their Sunday routines. Many were dolled up for church, others getting by with a twinkle in the eye, some with an aimless look or one compounded by trouble or ailment, and a few with obvious evil intent toward the rest.

This was the Ninth Ward, the back part, or at least further back. Black New Orleans largely. One of the areas of town that many had never seen. Even fewer had been on the other side of the Florida Avenue Canal.

Delery remembered a wearying series of ongoing questions once students and colleagues in Chicago learned after Katrina that he was a native New Orleanian, especially when he'd mentioned that he'd lived in the Ninth Ward.

"Why weren't those people in the Lower Ninth Ward living

on higher ground?" was one that required explaining that "upper" and "lower" were directional, not used geographically.

Even the simplest queries required a mini-lesson on the location of New Orleans between the river and the lake, as well as about the canals that ran through the city. There were exponentially more of them than in Venice, Italy. They were in place to pump rainwater back to the lake, if necessary.

The city had changed when he left with his dad in 1979, though. He'd never heard the term "Bywater" used as a kid, though it was one of the hot neighborhoods all over the international press now. Didn't make sense to him. Everyone in the city was by water. But, he bought into it too. Look where he was renting.

Despite the abandoned lots and having been away for over three decades, the neighborhood still felt familiar to him. Nowhere else does architecture look like that in New Orleans.

"I wonder what it's like across the Industrial Canal now. Fields of weeds? Many people back?"

Delery planned to take a drive over the bridge to see the Lower Ninth Ward for himself, but he'd read enough to know that, despite the media attention, little support had come. Mainly Brad Pitt's foundation and a few legitimate non-profits.

He hadn't expected to see so many empty lots on this side of the canal, though. He knew he wouldn't get caught up in looking around and miss the family house. It couldn't be forgotten. Right at the corner of Galvez and Poland. Across the wide busy Poland was a smattering of warehouses and marine businesses. That wouldn't change.

He looked off to the left instinctively at the Bartholomew intersection.

The Florida Projects were built on the river side of the Florida Avenue Canal decades ago as housing for whites, his dad had told him in Chicago when they were discussing

Cabrini-Green getting torn down there.

"Bobby, by the time we left New Orleans, the old white projects--St. Thomas, Iberville, and Florida--they were all black," he'd said. "At least people living in those could mix with everyone else. Look at the Desire Projects, though. They put a bunch of poor people in shoddy buildings that weren't fit for habitation the day the doors opened. Stuck in isolation between train tracks on left and right sides. I-10 on top. Florida Canal on the bottom. Limited socialization."

His voice had raised. "You know what that does to a person. You've studied it. What does it say? It says, 'Take a bus downtown where you make a lousy wage at your crappy job, if you can even get one, and when your shift's over go away to an isolated corner so we don't have to see you anymore.' New Orleans likes its black people in two contexts. Work for us or entertain us. White folks have a problem with black folks as just people. I'll be the first to say it."

Delery saw he was a block away. He knew his mother and brothers didn't live there anymore, or in New Orleans at all, but he'd grown up in this house during his formative years. A warehouse filled the entire block on the left. Memories from the houses along the right side filled him up.

It doesn't matter where you're from or where you've been. The house or structure where you were born and raised holds a special place. It alchemically transforms standard building materials into something magical.

The excitement built inside him. He knew coming back would be emotionally difficult. The family home was in the part of his memory where roads don't run. Delery didn't like them to run there anyway.

As he got closer, the yard seemed bigger and thicker than he remembered. "The owners must need to do some yard work," he said, finally pulling up in front.

His mouth dropped. Weeds of all types abounded. He was home, but home wasn't there.

Delery got out of his car, double-checked the street signs, and walked to the empty lot in disbelief. He saw red paint barely visible underneath the overgrowth. The only remaining part of the family house was the stoop. Three steps made of concrete. Left when the shotgun single was demolished and taken away.

"It's faded, but this is the red Dad painted when I was in first grade," Delery said.

He pushed the weeds back vigorously so he could sit on the top step. Delery didn't make a habit of crying, but he let loose and sobbed for a couple minutes.

He'd been in two worlds his whole life. His tender spot. What gave him perspective and experience beyond most people. It was also what could wound him to the quick like nothing else. Why he lived in two worlds. Not quite fitting in either. Wondering which person he was. Here he was at the source of it. Simultaneously close and far from his family.

"I need to get it out," he said to himself, "but not aloud."

"Dad and Mama married in February 1965. George Delery and Celeste Thomas. Made house in this spot on the other side of town from their families because both sides disapproved."

He wiped his eyes with the back of his hand.

"Mama was pregnant with Robert. The first one. He died when she was giving birth."

Delery didn't have a handkerchief or tissue, so he leaned off to the side, held the top of his nose between thumb and index finger, and blew his nose into the weeds.

"Marvin was born in 1966. He also would've been my older brother. Died when he was only three from sickle cell. Painful death."

Delery paused, thinking of his birthday a couple months

ahead.

"I was the oldest by happenstance. By accident. August 28, 1970. They used 'Robert' again. Looking back, I think it was too difficult for them to say it out loud, so I was always 'Bobby.'"

His hands were on his knees. He squeezed them.

"I was still a baby myself when Isaac was born in 1973. Looked so different from me. My little brother. Wonder what he's done with his life?"

Delery teared up again and promptly blotted with his hand.

"They had Curtis when I was in kindergarten. Would've been 1976. A toddler when Dad and Mama got divorced. I remember his eyes when Dad and I left. He knew somehow."

Delery made two fists and started to steadily knock his knuckles together.

"As part of the divorce settlement, Dad got me. Mama got Isaac and Curtis. We left the state. Dad got a job in Indiana. Union organizing job with UAW. At International Harvester. Went back and forth from Fort Wayne to Chicago a lot for work."

His knuckle tapping got stronger. Noise from their impact could be heard.

"Once a week, I wrote a letter to Mama, Isaac, and Curtis. Gave them to Dad to mail. Never got a reply. Stopped writing after 6th grade. Dad wouldn't allow long distance phone calls, so letters were all I had. But…they…they forgot about me."

His arms were now swinging and his fists were colliding with each other.

"Fuck, fuck, fuck. What did I do wrong, Mama? Dad said the three of you left New Orleans. Wouldn't tell me where. Said it was better that way. I was a freshman in high school then."

He violently slammed his fists together once before stopping.

"All these years. I never looked online. Figured if I was dead to them, what did it matter?"

Delery had been so deep in his release he was unaware of his surroundings. A mistake in any city, but definitely so in New Orleans.

He jolted when he saw three teenagers standing off to his right. He hadn't seen or heard them come around the corner. Each had a variation of long white t-shirt, black low-slung pants, and shoulder length dreadlocks. He thought they were young gangsters, and they knew it.

Delery rose and panicked. He tried to pull fear from his face and broke the awkward silence. "You guys didn't see all that shit, did you?" he asked. For all he knew, his lips had moved with his thoughts.

One of the trio brushed it off. "You don't have to say anything. Private ish. What you doing sitting out here, though?"

"This was where my house used to be," Delery said.

"You lived back here? C'mon. Naw."

Delery knew what was being implied, and his initial response to them meant he deserved it. "Yeah, I grew up here but moved away when I was still a kid. Before you guys were even born."

"Well, listen. We didn't mean to get up in your business, sir, but maybe you want to come to this," the spokesperson offered, handing Delery a postcard-sized promotion for a music show.

"This is you guys?" he asked. "And you don't have to 'sir' me. I appreciate the respect to a sad old man, though."

They all grinned.

"You're not that old. But, yeah, that's us. We're students at NOCCA, but the show's at the Musician's Village."

Delery was foggy. "I've never heard of either of those. Guess I have been away for a minute."

They schooled him on the high school arts center next to the river, which was actually near his apartment, and the Habitat for Humanity houses only blocks away, built for musicians after the flood.

They were sweet generous kids and their music sounded interesting, so Delery promised to catch their show the following Thursday. When they were about to part, one of the three who'd been silent so far, said with a sly grin, "I ain't gonna dap. Nothin' personal. But your knuckles, they ain't touchin' mine. Gotta keep 'em pretty for the trumpet. You dap like you're trainin' to beat Mayweather."

They all burst out laughing and made introductions.

"I've had a hell of a day. Nice to meet you guys. And sorry about my first response. Thanks for being cool about it," Delery said.

He was ready to head downtown. Took Poland to Claiborne and saw everything as expected along the way, except for an older woman walking slowly along the pedestrian part of the Claiborne overpass above the train tracks. She was dressed all in white, obviously on her way to church.

The peculiar thing was that she was carrying a large beer case almost half her size.

10

Hutch's appetite was kicking. Having the Chinese restaurant directly across the street in full view made his stomach worse. He was hoping it'd be open soon, so he could pick up some food and bring it back without anyone seeing him. Otherwise, time to start limping to a truck stop and catch a lift to Houston.

Traffic on Franklin was steady, usual for Sunday morning, but Hutch's attention casually drifted to the sidewalk directly below him. He jumped inside himself and barely kept from calling out. He'd been smacked like a nightmare.

"Shit. Granny got it?" he mouthed.

He was stunned to see a woman slowly pass beneath the window. She was old and moved like it. All in white from head to toe, blending beautifully with her black skin.

She was also unmistakably carrying the large Abita beer case that flew out the jeep window with Clint Olson. It had the large mark in the corner that Mr. C required of his bartenders for inventory, but was the money in it?

Hutch scrambled to the stairs, limping and dodging rubble, trying to keep from falling through the weak floorboards. Coughing the whole way. He hobbled downstairs and out the back, pulled himself over two chain link fences, and finally arrived at the sidewalk, adrenaline-filled.

Looking off to the right, he saw she'd crossed Derbigny and was passing through a group of people. Gliding as if her feet weren't moving, so small were her steps. She turned into a building.

Hutch took a few steps to read the posted sign. New Grace Tabernacle Full Gospel Baptist Church. He reversed his steps to go back upstairs and stand at the window in wait for her to come back.

Black churches and white churches are as dissimilar as a placid bath and a vigorous shower. Water in a completely different framework.

White churches are often pious somber affairs. They tend to have a macabre fixation on the book of Revelations or an unhealthy obsession with the prosperity principle, that wealth is ordained for the devout. All is rigid.

Typically, black churches are entirely different. Joy for the soul. Music for the ears and body. Blessings for the heart and mind. Also, performances from the pulpit like no other. Despite black culture being routinely co-opted and turned into weak tea for a white mainstream in the U.S., black churches largely haven't been touched. Why? Because it can't be pulled off.

This is definitely the case in New Orleans when black folks go churchin' and most definitely for those who do so at The Tab.

The Tab, usual nickname for the seven word version on the sign, had been around for two decades. It was nondescript from the outside. Not a house church or a storefront one. Not ostentatious either. In fact, it appeared almost fortress-like.

Miss Melba passed through the opened security fence and the door on the right held for her. There was a modest foyer with a greeter's desk on the left and an overflow room off to the side. Music was easily heard pouring through the walls.

She was known for being devout, so eyebrows raised high, elbows nudged, mouths dropped, and eyes popped when she glided through them all, carrying a beer case on her way to the sanctuary.

"Excuse me. Would you place a program in my hand?" she asked, announcing, "Only commodities inside. No devil brew in this box."

A kindly usher opened the door and led her to a seat in a

pew off to the right for latecomers. Actions by those who saw her echoed those in the lobby, with the addition of friends who greeted her by name, nodded with a smile, or gently squeezed her arm. Each time she repeated her pat response about commodities. Each time they affirmed in reply.

Miss Melba placed the box at her feet and joined in the service. Everyone was standing and most were swaying to the choir. Though the music was sublime, the four speakers mounted overhead on the sides blasted the voices and instruments at a level that would humble a rock club. It didn't bother Miss Melba. Her hearing had dropped off plenty over the years.

In front of her, there were twelve long rows divided in thirds by two aisles. Four short rows in back where she was standing were separated from the larger section by a wide aisle. At capacity, the church could seat upwards of 180 people.

The walls and ceiling were white. The carpet and pews were blue. All crisp in the post-disaster way that parts of the city looked like they'd just come out of the box.

The twenty-five members of the superchoir were singing in a hypnotic African-influenced call-and-response way. They were gathered along an elevated stage up four steps on one side of the pulpit. The drummer, keyboardist, organist, and percussionist were on the other. James Brown and the JB's would've taken a few pointers.

There were two large flat screen tv's on the wall behind them looping through announcements and motivational sayings. Two overhead banks of lights completed the balance.

All the high-tech equipment was in full force, except for air conditioning. Ladies were fanning themselves. Men were wiping their brows. There was a mix of the nicely dressed, many in white like Miss Melba, and the extremely casual. A few folks were stylin' in a major way, and one young man wore a t-shirt that read "Fallen Heroes" at the top and had pictures of Tupac and Biggie below. If folks had a little money, they were dressing fancy come Sunday. Hair was done no matter what.

The congregants were regular people of modest means, almost all from the surrounding neighborhood. Their lives were not easy or filled with creature comforts. For a few hours each Sunday they had a place that was theirs to help get through the week. Plus, the house was rockin'.

After the choir sang a song with the key line, "Let's go back to the old time days," slipping and sliding along the melody and chanting for over a quarter hour, Sister Pastor Yvonne Russell stood from her seat at the edge of the stage.

She clapped and raised her hands up along with everyone else. When she reached the pulpit, Sister leaned into the mic and said, "Good morning. So happy to see everyone today. But you know, we don't wanna go back to those old days, do we?"

Everyone either vigorously answered back, "No!" or at least shook their heads.

"That's right. We're walking through new days. Without Jesus, where we gonna be? In the grave, under the jail, under the grave, in the jail."

A wrinkled man called out, "Don't forget right on top of the grave."

Sister Pastor Russell announced the monthly Youth Spotlight winner, Fenny Kendrick. The fourteen year old was dressed in a white leotard and colorful tutu for her interpretive dance of a recorded praise song. She was filled with the Spirit and nervousness, but everyone was supportive of her twirling, particularly when she used her index fingers and thumbs to put her diamonds up to the sky. She was thanked with applause and a gift certificate.

Next, Sister Pastor announced the church's senior pastor. Though his given name was Terrell Jackson, he was known to all as Slow Prophet, or S.P. for short. Organ music and clapping in unison wove a carpet for his entrance, from a door behind the stage, up to the pulpit. He chastely embraced Sister Pastor Russell, looked out to the pews, and straightened his dashiki.

"It's a blessed Sunday. Greet those around you. Nobody's greeting you, then you hug yourself," he began in an understated way.

He was barely thirty-three but had the full husky voice of an older man. He wore black dress pants and sported black sneakers. A large watch on his left wrist was his only concession to modern fashion.

"Do I look like I'm ready to come correct?" he asked, nodding to the responses.

S.P. was a man whose weight and appearance fluctuated greatly depending on how many Big Buford's he'd had that week. He admitted as much by mentioning that the devil drove him to drive-thru, but the Lord made a long line that eventually S.P. gave up on.

All joined hands for prayer.

"Don't rob God," was S.P.'s call for the offering. Tithing envelopes were passed out. A line formed along each aisle, and two young boys waited in front for the newly filled envelopes to be placed in the containers that resembled flower pots.

Miss Melba thrust an empty left hand into her beer case, grabbed one of the money packets, inserted a tithing envelope into the case with her right hand, and discreetly tucked the money inside, writing nothing on the envelope. She was at church but wasn't foolish enough to think that mattered with the amount she had.

She less-discreetly carried the box of money with her and took her place in line, with the stuffed envelope on top of the refolded lid. Those who hadn't initially seen her come in went through the prescribed nudging, eyebrow raising, mouth dropping, and asides. She quietly repeated, "Only some commodities. No devil brew here," all the way to the stage.

One person responded to her more strongly than the others. He snorted like he'd heard the joke of all jokes, but not a funny one. His mouth hung slack like an imbecile. He flung his arms up, back down, then up again. He shook like a junkie quitting cold turkey.

The lady to his left smiled. "You've got the faith," she said.

The Holy Trinity was *not* the catalyst for his erratic movements, though. D-Day, so called because of his name David Day and the destruction he was prone to unleash, was in a quandary. He'd been trying to get his life right. His face was carved up with scars from several knife scuffles over his twenty-eight years. His mind was carved up by an upbringing far more violent.

D-Day started sweating. Here was a trial presenting itself. He'd heard on the street about a missing beer box of money, and it looked like the old lady standing in the aisle to his right had it.

"Hustler recognize hustler," he muttered.

His internal struggle was strong before seeing what Miss Melba held. He'd spent last night pulling the crutch hustle on tourists. It was too easy, especially on a Saturday night.

He'd limp around with one crutch for support. No one's scared of an invalid, so they'd let their guard down. D-Day would either swat them over the head with the crutch or use it from behind to choke. Whichever route, he could spend a few hours Saturday night and make a week's worth of cheese. At least $500.

The problem was that his conscience was weighing heavy on him. He was back in church for the first time in over a decade, and the temptation of all temptations was so close he could smell it.

The lines cycled through the tithers, including Miss Melba, and they all took their seats.

D-Day looked over his shoulder, so he knew where Miss Melba was sitting. She wasn't leaving before the end of the sermon. He knew that much.

Slow Prophet checked his watch. 11:50 a.m.

"This is from the book of James. Chapter 1, verse 8," he said, holding up his Bible. "A double-minded man is unstable in all his ways," he read.

For the next forty-five minutes, S.P. took that verse and stretched it, sliced it, soothed it, and diced it. He was masterful at his craft, his interweaving and referencing no lesser to the art of Escher or the compositions of Bach.

He always started the same way. "I'm just a man, a vessel filled up by Jesus. He took his time with me, so I gotta take my time with you. And how do I preach?" he asked.

"Slow!" they responded.

He smiled and nodded. "That's right. I start out slow until the Lord tells me to move, to cruise. Until then, can I take my time?"

"Keep it slow, Slow Prophet."

"I said, 'Can I take my time?' Mmm hmmm. Can you walk if you're cut in half? Hoppin' on one leg. Can you drive a car with only wheels on the left side? That car's tippin' over. Double-minded man's like that. Unstable." His words were drawn out, each syllable deliberated.

"Preach it, S.P.," a few called out.

"A double mind's not good for a man," he mused, pointing at his head. "Brings too much confusion. It'll mess with you. Tip you over. Make you hop so much you start crawlin'. This applies for you too, ladies. Oh yes. Can you put on those new jeans, the ones with the rhinestones on the back pockets and the little rips down the front, if they're cut in half? Would you step outside the nail salon if only your left hand's done?"

The woman of The Tab were aghast. "Of course not!"

"Yes, if you're not ready for the blessing, the blessing's…," he paused and gestured.

"Not ready for you," several said, completing the line.

Miss Melba and D-Day were responding to the sermon in opposite ways. She felt confirmation of her actions to come after church, that she was single-minded by faith. He, on the other hand, was even more torn by the minute.

"Look at your neighbor and tell 'em, 'No more double mind,'" S.P. encouraged. The congregation all earnestly repeated it to those around them.

"You gotta be mindful. If you're single-minded, He's got the power. I wish I had a witness in here."

Hands rose throughout the sanctuary. "C'mon, pastor."

"When's the last night you had a full night's rest? Double mind'll mess with you."

If a black man could have a sickly green pallor, it was D-Day.

Slow Prophet crouched, pulled out a handkerchief, and wiped his face.

"Time for ole S.P. to get movin'. You gotta move your mind. Gotta be mindful. Tell someone, 'I need some answers and I need some help.'" His request was repeated throughout the sanctuary. He started picking up the pace.

"Can't live life unstable. You need to rewind that double mind. Rewind it now," he exhorted. "Can I get a witness?"

Hands popped up again. S.P. squatted down.

"Cut in half's not pretty, is it? Not pretty on the inside either."

"Help us today" and "No sir" were heard throughout the room.

D-Day was ready to break. He had three ways to go. He could go crawling, clawing, and crying in repentance down the aisle. He could defiantly reject the sermon. Or he could find a third way. Whichever route, it needed to happen quickly.

He chose the latter, or actually, it chose him. "No more crutch hustle. No more stealin'. Get my mind stable. Alla that…after I get the box of money. Jesus want me to have it," he thought.

For the next few minutes, he listened only in a cursory way, responding to S.P. in whichever way his neighbors were. It seemed like he was in a dream. D-Day was planning.

The sound of drums and keyboard jolted him back to the sanctuary.

"You are coming out of your dark season," Slow Prophet stressed. He boomed, "Cain't nobody tip you over. Especially yourself. Look at your neighbors and tell 'em, 'Nobody's tipping me over. I'm…not…tipping…me…over…either!'" His last line was punctuated by musical stabs.

Heads shook from side to side and fingers wagged while everyone said the same thing to anyone within earshot.

With a fuzzy corrupted way of thinking, D-Day believed it was God's will that he get the money from Miss Melba. He'd initially thought Slow Prophet was preaching *at* him because of how the words cut, but now in his mind he'd twisted it to think the sermon was *for* him. The Father, Son, and the Holy Ghost wanted him to have that beer case. The twelve disciples too.

S.P. was now singing his sermon, each line alternating with its musical counterpart.

"A double mind's a devil mind."

Ta-ta-ta-boom. Ta-ta-da-boom.

"Don't pay no mind to devil mind."

Ta-ta-ta-boom. Ta-ta-da-boom.

A lady sitting midway back from the pulpit pulled out a tambourine from her purse and started shaking it.

"Can't preach like Peter, pray like Paul?"

Ta-ta-boom-boom. Ta-ta-boom-boom.

"Keep it stable, keep it strong."

Ta-boom-boom-boom. Ta-boom-ta-boom.

It was building higher. The music directly accompanied Slow Prophet. The congregants sang lines back to him.

"Kick the devil out your house. Put him out. Evict him now. Flip it over in your mind. Flip it, tip it, make it fine."

Throughout The Tab, people were up dancing, crying, smiling, and raising up their hands. In the midst of it all, Miss Melba kept a sharp eye on the beer case under her feet.

S.P. swung out his arm and checked the time. 12:35 p.m. He signaled to the musicians, and they all took it down. Drums dropped out. Keyboard played a contemplative hymn. S.P. spoke softly. For about five minutes, it was mellow.

By another five, the full-throttle energy was back.

In five more minutes, it was down again. Time for the altar call.

"I fell down, but I got up. How about you?" S.P. beseeched.

Three songs were played. Half a dozen people, young and old, came forward.

Slow Prophet asked everyone to put their hands forward while he prayed for those who'd come to the altar. Many of the congregation prayed aloud right with him.

D-Day was steadily checking on Miss Melba by this point. He saw her reach down and lift up the beer case. She was about to leave.

"Can't nobody think I'm following," he reasoned. He stepped into the aisle, quickly walked to the back, and headed to the door. He was in front of her, so he seemed less suspicious.

Out into the foyer he went and finally returned to the sunlight. He didn't know if she'd driven and was in parked in the lot, so he lurked near the door.

Miss Melba arrived outside shortly after. She squinted in

the light and saw a rough mangled looking fellow look at her out of the corner of his eye. Mistakenly presuming it was a judgmental fish-eye, she said, "Just commodities, young man." Feeling frisky of spirit after the sermon, she added, "For my cats, Moses and Allen Toussaint."

Surprise flashed in D-Day's eyes, but he realized she was trying to play him in some way.

"Hustler recognize hustler," he mused.

"Allen Toussaint, huh?" he responded aloud, thinking she was also making up that part.

"Goodness, yes," she said. "Too-Too loves his treats. In a dignified way, of course. After all, he's quite…" She stopped herself. "Excuse me, but I have a bus to catch."

D-Day was frozen in place.

11

Miss Melba walked in her slow gliding way out to the sidewalk, eyes peeking over the top of the beer case she held. When the traffic signal changed in her favor, she crossed, stepped through the grassy neutral ground, and passed along the two lanes on the other side, as well.

"Alvin, your little Chickie's going downtown," she said to the sky.

She was now directly across the street from The Tab, at a bus stop for the #57. Now that she was retired, she didn't venture out much, especially not to Canal Street. Had she been leaving directly from home, she'd have caught the #80 on Louisa, like she used to do to get to work.

No schedule was posted, just an RTA sign stating the bus number, but that didn't matter. Public transportation in New Orleans was irregular and inefficient. Only the carless or those who had no other options put themselves at its mercy. So, wait they did.

"Who knows how long this bus might be," thought Miss Melba. There was no bus hut or bench, so she placed the heavy case on the sidewalk and sat on it, facing the street.

There was a flurry of activity inside the Metro PCS store behind her. The Sunday clerk and store manager were stomping through the tiny place, taking in how much of their stock had been stolen overnight. The thieves had trimmed the alarm wires and entered from the back door, so they'd had their run of the store to walk out with several smartphones. Behind the store, on Derbigny, were a barbershop and tire shop, but both were closed.

Miss Melba began to smell the wafting scent of Chinese

food on her right. It put her in the mood for her eventual destination downtown, including her former secret indulgence. The #57 wouldn't take her to its front door, but once she got to Rampart and Canal it'd only be a short walk away.

Chinese Inn was set back from the street to allow for limited parking. It was a to-go restaurant, so cars were continually pulling in and out. Plenty of walk-up business too. Despite the name, the restaurant was run by a Vietnamese family. The Vietnamese not only ran most of the Asian restaurants of all kinds in the area but also many of the corner markets or hole-in-the-walls that featured spicy boiled shrimp and crawfish in season.

The building and signage were crude and no-nonsense but completely effective. Simple rectangular white-washed one-story building fronted by a large red add-on sign supported by red posts. Large white Chinese looking English letters unevenly spelled out the restaurant's name. Various menu items were handwritten in red on the building itself.

Chinese Inn was typically closed on Sundays, but exorbitant medical bills for the Tran family's oldest son had them scrambling for funds. Extra hours at their two restaurants were in effect. The farce of what health care in the country had become over the past twenty years was only slightly met by the events about to play out at the bus stop.

Hutch had seen Miss Melba cross the street. He was already free of his hiding spot and back out to the sidewalk, advancing toward her, coughing the whole way. He was on The Tab side of Franklin, and she was only four lanes of traffic away.

Hutch also noticed a rough looking guy with a beatific expression in profile already crossing Franklin up ahead, so seeing no oncoming traffic, he did the same, ending up on the sidewalk directly in front of Chinese Inn. D-Day was half a block away in front of a parking lot protected by a barbed wire-topped chain link fence. Miss Melba was waiting for the bus in a fairly equidistant spot between the two of them.

She noticed both men heading her way, the one after church who she thought was silently accusing her of toting beer and another twice his age who was hobbling along.

"Goodness, this reminds me of Marlon's game," she said to herself, thinking of Marlon Batiste, her neighbor on Clouet. Most every day but Sunday he was out playing chess with anyone else who joined in. He'd built a structure supported by three posts that extended the roof line of his little house across the sidewalk to the grassy strip before the street. Set up his table and chairs on the sidewalk under the overhang so that they could play in the shade while they nursed a few beers. Older black men congregated on neutral grounds throughout the city, under trees when they could. Batiste's was merely a version of the tradition.

"What makes chess fair is both players knowing the strengths and weaknesses of each piece," she thought. "Real life is different. Sometimes what you think is a pawn is instead a queen. Or vice versa."

The scars on D-Day's face were pulsing in anticipation.

"Jesus want me to have it. No more tippin' over," he muttered.

"Can't believe the money turned up like this," Hutch coughed. Watching D-Day, "Young brother better sleep on it. If I gotta do him, I sure will," came out in one long hack. He wasn't armed, so he meant using his bare hands.

D-Day read Hutch's intensity as if he could hear him.

"Nigga you betta walk on by. Soulja comin' your way. A Holy soulja," he gritted through his teeth. He'd not brought his gun or knife to church but always kept a screwdriver in his pocket just in case.

Wind gusts began to kick up dirt and shake the trees. A storm system was moving through, but it had split in two, bringing thunderstorms to the other side of the lake and river. Most of New Orleans was experiencing only a brief respite from the summer heat.

Both Hutch and D-Day were a few steps from Miss Melba. Both locked their jaws and held them forward. Both narrowed their eyes and held their shoulders high in the wind.

Within seconds, they all formed an odd triangle. Hutch leaning in on the left, D-Day on the right, and the seated Miss Melba in the middle.

The two men were mean muggin' each other, not focusing on their common object of interest.

"Son, this thing ain't for you," Hutch said.

D-Day smacked his own chest. "I'm doin' the Lord's work. Who you, buster?"

"We got a problem, sucker?" Hutch asked.

Miss Melba knew to expect this sort of thing. She had two sons. A husband too, up until recently. She'd spent her whole life around men who were often not treated as men. She knew how to handle it. "Excuse me, men," she said. "There's no need to beef. You don't even know each other."

She looked directly at Hutch. "You look hungry, baby. Are you hungry?" She didn't comment on how much he stunk.

Hutch was taken aback.

"Yes, ma'am, but that don't matter. What's gonna happen is…"

She held up a hand.

"See that Chinese place? Why don't you get some food in your belly. It'll make your mind better. Spiciness will help your throat. Don't go to Turner's over there. I hear something's shady with the recipes."

Both men nodded. She reached out, touched Hutch's arm, and kept her hand in place.

"Looks like you haven't slept. No bus coming yet. Go get

some food. Won't take long."

Although Hutch had planned to first take down D-Day and then strong arm the beer case out from under her, Miss Melba convinced him to follow her directions when she opened her big white purse and slightly withdrew an object. Both men were stunned to see her hand firmly clenched around the grip and trigger of a gun, though D-Day thought it was a Taser.

"I don't need to take this all the way out, do I?" she asked. "My husband taught me if it comes out, you use it."

D-Day considered grabbing his screwdriver. She turned to him, knowing somehow.

"Why don't you go with him, baby? The sweet & sour chicken's supposed to be good. Don't worry about me. I'm not going anywhere. Don't turn down no food," she said, smiling gently and handing both D-Day and Hutch $10 bills with her other hand.

She didn't let loose of the gun until they were midway to the restaurant. Her hand started to tremble. Miss Melba looked upward.

"Alvin, you said there'd never be use again for that starter's pistol once Zekey ran his last track meet senior year. You old fool. But look at me. Biggest fool of all to think I can pull this off. Can't by myself. Sure can't take this out of my purse, then they'd know what it is."

She closed her eyes and thought. After finishing, the trouble lifted from her eyes.

"Too many of our people keep losing a game they don't know how to play. Not me. Won't bleed me. Not today," she said.

NOPD officers Bourgeois and McCoy drove past Miss Melba. They'd spent the morning fruitlessly looking for a whiter-than-white man in a black church and otherwise cruising around the neighborhood searching for an Abita

Amber beer case full of money. Hassling Bobby Delery too.

Word had spread among the rank and file that Dominic Cavallari would pay $50,000 for the box of money, $60K if his employee came with it. A former boxer named Raymond "Hutch" Pate. It was like a scavenger hunt for cops.

Though Sunday mornings were slow for 911 calls, most of the slim number were ignored to focus on finding the money. Officers were riding alone. NOPD was in the midst of major attrition by felony or flight, dropping their ranks by getting themselves locked up or moving on to greener pastures. Partnerless patrolling made typical policework dangerous, but the majority thought it advantageous to go solo for the money search.

Bourgeois and McCoy felt their chances were better for capturing Pate and the money as a team, so they doubled up. Bourgeois was a born and raised local who wore a pompadour like Elvis. McCoy was an Okie who'd moved down a few years before. He sported short moussed-up bangs like it was still the late 80's. Both had bright swatches of red on their necks and noses from the sun. Splinter-colored hair and splinter-minded beliefs. Bourgeois was all lips. McCoy was all nose.

Though Miss Melba was sitting on the exact item they were looking for, it didn't register to either of them. Neither did her attire.

"Goddamn, Bourg. Look at this. Sunday morning and grandma's out buyin' beer. No food, just beer. Shee-it," said the indignant McCoy.

"Probably with food stamps too. The stores around here don't care. Winos keep 'em in business. Bet they gave her a free phone too. Fucking country isn't ours anymore," replied Bourgeois.

Stuffed to their chins with aggrievement, on they went, not noticing that the broad-shouldered man who turned around after paying for his food order was the same one pictured on the video camera still they both had seen on their phones.

"Thank you, Jesus," praised Miss Melba. She looked back to the right and saw Hutch and D-Day discreetly trying to move behind a parked car while watching to make sure she was sitting at the bus stop. Though she didn't know it, D-Day was thinking that he had a couple outstanding warrants hanging over him, and Hutch knew his fake passport alone would get him put away for ten to fifteen years.

"Fight fire with fire," she said and jolted as if she'd been asleep.

She reached into her purse, remembering the object she'd bought a few weeks ago in case she needed to relight her gas stove burners when Entergy's power grid failed again during another summer rain shower. After a couple thumb flicks, an inch high flame steadily emitted from the cheap lighter.

"Well, alright," she said, pleased, letting loose her thumb and closing her hand.

After a few minutes, the two men received their food and brought it over, together but separate. They were uncomfortable adversaries, and it was clear they hadn't said two words to each other in the meantime.

Both of them stood while they ate, Hutch on the left and D-Day to the right of Miss Melba. Privately, Hutch planned to take care of business when he finished his fried rice. D-Day, on the other hand, thought it was God's will that he eat half of the sweet & sour chicken, throw the rest of the steaming food into the bigger man's face, and pull the beer case out from under the old lady at last.

Miss Melba looked and took them both in as if for the first time. She saw Hutch's unkempt short afro, his look of messy desperation. D-Day was altogether different. He looked tough with his shaved head and scars but seemed like he was still receiving blessings at church.

There was no sign of the bus yet.

"I only have to stay one step ahead of them, like Marlon's chess game," she thought. "Just keep checking. Make *them* stay on the defense."

She looked back and forth. "Now, men," she said, opening her hand to show the lighter.

"It only takes a spark to get a fire. Am I wrong? This here lighter is full of fluid." She flicked the flint and held the button to bring it to life.

"It works fine. Quick light." She held her hand down by her side a scant inch from the beer case of money. Hutch and D-Day stopped eating. They were speechless.

"Now, men, these, ah, commodities in the box. I don't need trouble. If I think I'm gonna get it because of the commodities, then it all goes up in flames. Problem solved."

"Ma'am, you don't need to do nothin' drastic," Hutch urged and extended an open hand. D-Day nodded.

Miss Melba let the flame drop but kept her hand down next to the box.

"No, I expect I don't. But I will if I need to. Understood?" she asked. "Men, here's the bus at last."

They each boarded the bus in reverse order of age. Hutch and D-Day weren't letting Miss Melba out of their sight. The driver wouldn't allow food on board, so the go-containers, silverware, and plastic bags were casually tossed to the street.

After Hutch paid his $1.25, he found Miss Melba seated on the front left, holding the box on her lap. The lighter was still in her hand, right up next to the box. All the seats around her were taken. The seats on the front right-hand side were flipped up to accommodate the wheelchair of an older man with a beret, tortoise-shell glasses, and goatee. There were a few standing in the middle, holding the safety straps to keep their balance.

It was Sunday and many were heading downtown, either for work or play.

Hutch and D-Day took two available seats in the back left corner next to each other. Away from Miss Melba's calming influence, their mutual animosity rose again.

D-Day recognized Griot Sam's voice carrying through the bus from his wheelchair.

"All these young people moving here, they're coming from other places. We live here. We're *from* here. So why do they wanna make our place like their place…that…they…left?"

"Keep on, Sam" rang out from the middle seats. Another person said, "Aw, leave 'em alone." The 1/4 of the bus who were white newcomers in their twenties shrunk deep into their seats or were blissfully unknowing while engaged by their iPods.

"Two words – Manifest Destiny. It's in their blood. Back in the old days, it was all about taking land and preaching Jesus. So they said. My Jesus said nothing about taking Indian land."

There were a growing number of "Mmm hmm's" and giggles, along with the nervous faces who had never experienced anything like this and were starting to worry that a race war was about to break out on the #57. Hutch's coughing in back could also be heard.

"Manifest Destiny. But these white folks – sorry, white folks, I gotta tell it how it is – they don't believe in Jesus," he accused.

The murmuring from the churchgoers resounded like a beehive buzz.

"They don't care too much about the land either. Sure, they're buying up lots of houses, but they're colonizing in a different way. Make no mistake, they *are* colonizers. They're cultural colonizers!" he hollered.

Griot Sam gestured out to St. Claude, where the bus was almost to the Elysian Fields stop.

He scoffed. "Look at this. A new restaurant. Korean-Creole. But not Korean run. Definitely not Creole run. No Koreans and no Creoles working there. That's something, isn't it? One more instance of white folks cooking other people's food. Trying to make New Orleans like the place they left. White people hybrid food. We know who gets left out. Without African-Americans, this city wouldn't look the same, talk the same, or taste the same. Man, they're happy to push us out. That's some shit. Okay, enough from me."

"If that ain't true, grits ain't groceries," said the woman next to Miss Melba.

After the stop, the #57 was filled to limited standing room.

None of them paid attention to the chalky passenger who slipped out the back exit door, wincing from the pain of his broken nose and sore elbow. Cheeks and eyes weren't feeling much better. Tyler Dolan had been grappling with confusion ever since waking up sore alongside an unfamiliar house on an unfamiliar street.

"Why was I there? Why did that guy try to get me while I walked home? Who was it the cops were looking for, all the squad cars I saw racing around after I snuck out of the church basement? All that because of my graffiti? Maybe Toes needs to retire," he said while slinking toward home. Even the wind couldn't resuscitate his depressed moustache.

Up until then, Hutch and D-Day hadn't exchanged words on the bus, only hot-tempered mad doggin' energy.

D-Day looked at the older man. "Whatchu gon' do with a box a paper? You raggedy. Smell nasty too. Jesus want me to have it. I fell down, but I got up."

Hutch's stare was hot enough to solder metal. "Shut your ass up 'fore you eat your tongue," he hissed.

The people sitting near them quickly got up, not only because the bus was almost to its destination of Rampart and

Canal.

"Pit bulls raised me. Turn you out, bitch. I'm a grown-ass man. Ain't divided no more, neither," said D-Day louder than before.

Not a soul was facing Hutch and D-Day, so they heard Hutch say, "Step off. Don't you threaten me again," but no one saw him act with lightning speed while he spoke.

"Callin' out your wolf ticket. I'm fi'in' to…" started D-Day, reaching for his screwdriver, but he didn't finish.

First, Hutch unhooked his belt and pulled it fully loose in one quick motion. He snapped it across D-Day's mouth. While the younger man was stunned, Hutch moved behind him and looped the belt twice around his neck, pulling firmly with all the force he'd built up from the day's anger and frustration.

In barely over two minutes, D-Day was dead, the second New Orleans death of the day. It would later be ruled a suicide as not to up the homicide count. Hutch left the belt around D-Day's neck and pushed him to the floor before filing off the bus with the others, ready to get the beer case back from Miss Melba.

The bus driver checked the time. It was 1:28 p.m.

12

Bobby Delery woke up to the chime of church bells. It was noon and exhaustion had caught up with him. He'd been unintentionally cat-napping in his car on St. Philip and Claiborne for over an hour. Notebook and pen were still in his lap.

In the meantime, New Orleans was New Orleans. Dirty dealing and sweet loving. Heartwarming kindness and soul-breaking cruelty.

Delery was parked in this spot for a reason. He was hungry before, but now even as sweaty, wrinkly, and drowsy as he was, it took a back seat to his rumbling stomach.

He was shaking off the cobwebs of sleep next to Roosevelt's Black Pearl. The food was his favorite in town as a kid. He was hoping that remained the case decades later.

When he stepped inside and scanned the room, it was generally as he recalled it. Small place. No frills. A few pictures on the walls. Three little tables along the left wall. Right side full of chafing dishes, cafeteria style. An aroma that took him way back.

A friendly-faced woman stepped over to help him and said, "Good morning."

"Good morning. I haven't been here for a few years. Same way to order?" he asked.

New Orleans was in line with Mexico and South America in that saying, "Good morning" was acceptable until at least 2 p.m.

"Sure. You just tell me what you want. I fill up this container. Today, we got stewed chicken, butter beans, fried chicken, mac & cheese, okra stew, greens, and…"

Delery stopped her. "Thank you, ma'am. I'll have the butter beans and greens. Do you have cornbread?"

She answered while ladling the food into a go-container. "No, not on Sundays. Bread pudding today."

"Oh, okay. I'll be back another day for cornbread, then. I'm eating in, by the way."

After checking to make sure he didn't want anything else, she handed him the container and plastic utensils before speaking to the elderly man behind the cash register. "$8.00," she said.

As Delery was paying, pleased at the price for the heaping portions, he asked the man, "Are you Mr. Roosevelt? My dad used to bring me here as a kid."

A lived-in voice replied. "I am indeed. Thanks for stopping in. Hope you like it."

Delery spent around twenty minutes taking care of his appetite for the whole day. The butter beans were nothing less than triumphant, better than he'd remembered. While he ate, a steady amount of people filed in, placed their orders, and left with their food. Men for the most part. A couple older ones were drinking at the little bar through a connecting doorway.

Delery thanked the lady and Mr. Roosevelt with a satisfied smile and went back out into the heat.

His parents felt the French Quarter was no place for a child, so back in the 1970's he'd only been through there a few times. Club Big Easy was on Bourbon, between St. Louis and Toulouse, Commander Jones had told him.

"If I can't find Bourbon Street, may as well go back to Chicago," Delery said.

After finding a parking spot on Dauphine near Matassa's, Delery checked his notebook. "I'm to speak with Dom Cavallari," he said, "the same guy who's trying to find the money before the police."

By the time he walked to St. Ann, he could hear where Bourbon was, so he made a left. When he got to Bourbon, he could see it became residential off to the left. He took a right.

Though it was midday on Sunday, Bourbon Street was coming to life. Everything from zydeco to a cover band playing "Hotel California" to a karaoke version of Madonna's "Borderline" to traditional jazz to modern pop and much more were heard booming from the clubs in just the first few blocks he walked.

Bourbon was a through-way for traffic that time of day, so the street wasn't awash with crowds, but the sidewalks were.

"Got to town yesterday. It's my first time on this street, but the criminologist in me is saying there have to be felons from several states out here. Probably a bunch of outstanding warrants too," he said to himself, taking in and sizing it all up. The crowd was taking pictures with their phones, drinking, or both.

Shortly after, he crossed the Toulouse intersection and saw a hotel on the right, which led his gaze to the left. There it was. A few doors down. Club Big Easy.

The barker out front was holding a drink special sign. A cover band was onstage playing a Bon Jovi song Delery had happily forgotten. A few people were dancing but most were standing in assorted oafish ways with drinks of an unnatural red color in long clear plastic containers that resembled the bell of a trumpet.

Delery walked past the bouncer, across the dance floor, and up to the bar. He was stopped before he got there.

"Hey darlin'. Want a Big Easy? It's the house drink. Otherwise, 2 for 1 on domestics," said a young waitress with a Club Big Easy shirt tied above her belly. She spoke as if she'd repeated those lines thousands of times.

"No, thanks. I'm here to see Dom Cavallari," he replied.

She got a sick look on her face and was about to respond.

Delery held up a hand. "Commander Jones from NOPD sent me."

She walked to the bar like she was on death row and relayed the message to the bartender while both of them stared at the intruder. Max, the bartender, was wearing a wireless mic. He called the second floor office.

"Yeah, what?" answered the voice on the other end.

Max took a deep breath. "Mr. C, sorry to bother you, but there's a guy down here to see you," he said cautiously.

"What the fuck did I tell you? All the shit I'm dealing with right now. No. Fuck no. I don't have time for this," Cavallari barked.

"That's fine. I'll tell him you're busy, but he said Commander Jones from NOPD sent him."

"Fuck," Cavallari huffed. "Alright, send him up."

Johnny, Cavallari's only henchman for the time being, had been out driving around Robertson and Claiborne with the Russians, hoping for a sign of Hutch. They were eating steak at Canal Place before heading back out on the search. The second floor of the club wasn't open yet, and Cavallari was the only one upstairs.

Delery walked over to the closed office door, as instructed, and knocked.

"Bobby Delery here to see Dom Cavallari," he announced.

The man he saw once the door opened had messy thick hair and rumpled clothes. Sloppy looking splints on his left pinky and ring fingers.

"What can I do for you, detective? I've already spoken to NOPD," he said.

"I bet you have," thought Delery, though he said aloud, "I'm actually a criminologist helping out the police because of the, uh, severity of the situation."

Cavallari scoffed. "It wasn't nearly as much money as the media made it out to be. Nothing more than a few deposits that two of my employees saw fit to steal. Sloppy too. They just threw it in a beer case. We have insurance. It's covered."

Delery pushed. "I'd like to review the video footage. I assume you have security cameras throughout this place."

Cavallari jousted. "The main console was on the fritz, and we hadn't gotten it fixed."

Delery nodded. "One of your employees involved in the theft was found dead on the Robertson overpass this morning. Most likely shortly after it happened. A guy named Clint Olson."

"I heard. That sounds like Hutch wanting to keep all the money for himself."

Delery sighed. "What was Hutch wearing when he left here?" he questioned.

"Lemme see," Cavallari said to allow time to think up a few whoppers. He didn't want this do-gooder he'd never seen before anywhere near Hutch or the money. He'd make a call about Commander Jones too.

Cavallari started in. "I'm pretty sure he was wearing a purple, green, and gold visor; neon green t-shirt; and a few strands of Mardi Gras beads. Saggy pants too. He walks with a limp. War injury. Has bad smoker's cough." The club manager smiled privately. "Good luck finding him with that description," he thought.

"It looked like all the employees downstairs were dressed in black or wearing t-shirts with the club's name on them," Delery said.

"Normally, sure, but we were having a Mardi Gras night on Saturday," lied Cavallari.

"This is too easy," he thought.

He waited until Delery stopped writing in a notebook. "If this helps, his real name's Raymond Pate. I don't know what

Hutch means. Probably from Starsky & Hutch. He's a big dude. Used to be a boxer."

Delery asked a few more questions, received a few more runaround answers, and ended the interview. He needed to get his mind focused on what he knew about the case. Walking helped him think, but Bourbon clearly wasn't the best street for that.

"Club Big Easy robbed of almost a million by two employees. Raymond 'Hutch' Pate and Clint Olson," he said softly. "They must've been on the run from Cavallari's people when Olson got killed. What's the connection to the blood trail I saw below the overpass?"

He turned on St. Louis, walking past a block full of unmemorable shops and restaurants.

"Whoever Cavallari answers to is after the money. NOPD's after the money, but a bunch of officers must be searching for Cavallari's sake. I imagine Hutch is long gone. Maybe there's another accomplice."

Delery continued across Royal. The courthouse took up the entire block on his right. Omni Royal hotel was on his left.

"What can I find that all the others aren't already picking up on?" he asked.

After admiring the Napoleon House building at the corner, he took a right on Chartres. A tour guide had a semi-circle of people grouped around her on the sidewalk. She was an older Creole woman, all charm, diction, and no-nonsense.

"Only drunks and the simple-minded disrespect these historic buildings. I know there's nobody like that in this group. Our next stop's the hotel across the street where quadroon balls used to be held. Follow me," she directed.

Delery found himself taken aback by the beauty of the architecture, contrasting the low-slung French Quarter to the hotels and office buildings that towered from a few blocks away.

He saw some better looking restaurants, though the shops seemed geared toward women. He was about to turn right at Bienville but saw an unexpected hand-painted sign reading Crescent City Books.

"A bookstore two blocks from Bourbon Street," he exclaimed. "I'll go back to the case shortly, but this'll help me clear my head. A brief stop."

Delery didn't realize there were actually seven bookshops in the Quarter, so the one solely symbolized the dichotomy of things to him. He strode with purpose, stopped at the front door, amused at the number of signs trying to regulate simple manners, and entered.

A handful of people were browsing. A bookish-looking fellow was pricing stacks he was taking out of boxes. Delery didn't recognize the music playing. It sounded modern, but not a brand-new kind of modern.

He walked past the prints and leather books to the rear, taking it all in. Passing back through the front, he followed the stairs up to the second floor, turning back to look at the view down below. At the top, he saw a good amount of fiction but was first drawn to the section by a window labeled "African-American History And More."

He flipped through a few books and tucked a cheap copy of Robert Deane Pharr's "Giveadamn Brown" under his arm. As he made his way to the titles face up on a couple tables, he was struck by the woman browsing in Philosophy.

"I'm a sweaty wrinkled mess right now. No way to clean up," he thought.

Delery turned to the first table. While adding new-but-discounted copies of "The Getaway" by Jim Thompson and "The Heat's On" by Chester Himes to the Pharr book, he thought about the browser. Criminology was a blend of psychology, sociology, and law enforcement. He regularly studied people through that lens, but this was different.

As he continued casually flipping through the table titles, Delery thought about the little that he'd seen and could conclude.

"Unique grace and poise. Seems intelligent and serious. About 5'8". Fresh-faced beautiful woman with a mocha complexion. Dressed nicely but casually. Sun dress, flats, stylish earrings, and necklace. Pepper spray hanging from her purse. Mid-to-late 20's. Hair pulled into a little knot in the back."

He turned around to catch her discreetly looking at him. She turned her head quickly.

Delery knew that many of those in the Quarter were tourists in town for only a brief interlude before returning to their regular lives. Chances were good she was too. He'd spent the morning going through a range of emotions, though, especially back where the family home used to be. Although he didn't look his best, she was obviously special. He had to meet her.

"I want to hear her voice. Know a little more about her. And those long legs," he continued.

She was now in Fiction, directly across him in profile. Saw him see her and didn't mind it. He took a few steps.

"Hey, how's it going?" Delery asked.

She smiled a reserved knowing smile and his legs got weak, but when she opened her mouth nothing came out.

Three possibilities seemed plausible to him. #1 She was shy and soft-spoken. #2 She was as nervous as he was. #3 She had no interest in him.

"So, are you visiting New Orleans?" he tried again.

One more time her reply was mute, as if the words couldn't find their way out.

"I apologize for disturbing you. Say, do you happen to know what music was playing downstairs?" he said, expecting to walk away next.

The voice he heard at last had a light New Orleans accent. It was reserved and sensitive. Her opinions were strong and obviously thought through. It was bliss to him.

"Yes, it's called 'Music for 18 Musicians' by Steve Reich. Some call it his signature piece. That's my thing, minimalist music. There's a lot of junk out there that calls itself minimalist, but I'm into Reich, Philip Glass, Johann Johannsson. Composers like that."

Delighted to hear her open up, Delery asked, "Do you compose?"

She responded like she'd been waiting for someone to ask. "Oh, no. I play piano, though. Paint expressionist art too, but no one will ever see *that*." She paused.

Delery felt like maybe he'd pushed it. "I'm going to pay for my books, but it was nice talking. I just moved back to town, and it's been a rough morning, so this was nice. My name's Bobby."

Her eyes sparkled. "I just got back too. About six months ago. I went to school in Baltimore. Lived up there for a while. I was ready to be away from New Orleans, but you know what? After ten years, I was surprised that I really missed home."

He was feeling more comfortable. "I've been away since I was nine. Listen…." He started to stumble a bit. "You're really striking and I…sorry, I'm talking under your clothes."

She smiled again. This time her mouth was closed for the wordless reply.

He tried again. "I'd like to see you again. Could I get in touch by email?"

She softly passed along her email address, which began with the letters "es." Delery jotted it down in his notebook.

"Are the "es" your initials?" he asked.

"Yes. My name's Ellis Smith," she said even softer than before.

Ellis seemed as enigmatic to him as when they first started talking. He still didn't know exactly where he stood, so he said, "Delery's my family name. Bobby Delery. See you, Ellis," shook her hand, and took the twenty-five steps down to the ground floor.

He overheard the bookseller responding to a phone query with, "We're open for another three hours and fifteen minutes. Close up at 5 o' clock on Sundays."

Delery paid for his books, left, and wandered to Decatur, taking it to Canal. His range of emotions for the day broadened further. He kept thinking about Ellis Smith and how he couldn't wait to see her again.

The French Quarter transforms based on time of day, location, and weather. Even adjacent blocks are different from their neighbors. Canal Street's energy reminded Delery of Michigan Avenue in Chicago, but far different. A Caribbean budget version.

In New Orleans, what's called loitering elsewhere is a way of life. It isn't criminalized but instead celebrated. People are public. The concept of streetcorner men means nothing. NOLA is a streetcorner city.

Delery stood at Decatur and Canal, alternating his thinking about how he'd next proceed on the case with thoughts of Ellis. He'd planned to watch the world go by, but the world at hand was stopped and honking. Traffic was backed up for blocks on his side of Canal, while there were very few cars on the other side, heading toward the river.

It was time to walk back to the car, but through the honking he heard a loud raspy coughing. He turned and saw a sight all the way across Canal that gave him pause.

"Wait a minute!" he exclaimed.

Traffic wasn't budging. He darted through the cars, across the neutral ground, and all the way to the sidewalk. The man was now a block ahead of him.

13

Hutch stepped out of the bus. His energy was up. He was ready to get the money.

"No more messin' 'round," he muttered amidst a coughing fit.

He scanned the crowd of people all around him next to the Saenger Theatre. No sign of the lady in white. No sign of the beer case.

"She can't have got too far," he said, turning back toward the direction they'd come from.

All of a sudden, the three dozen or so people milling about erupted.

Hutch turned back to see the sky filled with money. In the wash of the wind, bills were soaring and dipping, fluttering and stuttering.

"I gotta $100 bill!" shouted a heavyset woman who shoved it into her bra and went back to jumping for more.

Cars were stopping in the middle of the street. Their drivers and passengers joined the multitudes running from every direction to Rampart and Canal. A giddy man with a cowboy hat and conference lanyard that read "AICPA; Bounce Sanford; Casa Grande, AZ" said, "What a great place, this New Or-leenz."

Stunned at what he saw in front of him, the bus driver called out, "It's raining money!" as he joined the masses.

Bodies were banging into bodies. People climbing over each other. Arthritis was temporarily healed while the elderly dove and contorted themselves. Children turned into Olympic level gymnasts.

One person moved away from the fray. With commotion

behind her, cars stopping around her, and people running past her, she wasn't looking back.

"Jesus, take me to the river," Miss Melba said. Like a little engine that could, she crossed the street slow and steady, holding the heavy beer case. She made a left, heading to the foot of Canal Street and the mighty Mississippi.

She was the source of the mayhem. Like using a smoke bomb to deflect attention, she'd left the bus, taken a few steps, placed the beer case on the ground, kneeled and opened it, pulled bands off of two packets of money, and thrown it all upward with both hands as high as she could muster.

200 $100 bills had gone aloft like that. Before the stampede happened, she secured the box and left the scene, not waiting to see where Hutch was.

By the time he spotted Miss Melba on the other side of the street, she was stepping across Roosevelt Way.

Hutch hobbled after her but was having a worse time of it than before. His banged-up knee had worsened on the bus trip. Now that he was beltless, he had to grab a handful of denim at the pocket and keep pulling up to prevent his jeans from drooping so much he'd stumble. The mold had settled into his lungs, and he had repeated bouts of hacking. Plus, he had to wade through the crowd getting his money, but he let his elbows fly and shoved with his free hand.

He pulled himself across Canal while a party of sorts had developed. Most of the money had been grabbed, and people were gathered talking about it and what they were going to do with it.

"Goddamn. I'm out here grindin' and my money's flyin' away," he said to the clouds.

He kept Miss Melba in general eyeshot, about a block and a half ahead of him.

Canal was a street to shop, to see, and be seen for many

black high-schoolers and those in their twenties.

Miss Melba walked past two of them leaning against a shoe store between Carondelet and St. Charles.

The taller one was chastising the other, who was making sure his hi-top fade was tight.

"Where she at?"

"C'mon, Shoes. Lyric text me. She in one-a them women stores. She be along soon."

"I'ma spit some bars, son. Keep it official. Sixteen bars of my game, these bitches be shakin' they cakes all over the street," bragged Blue Shoes.

"Naw, prolly jes that old lady with her beer box," scoffed Stink, slowly doing a dance move like he was aged.

Blue Shoes came back hard. "Lyric make a nigga nut for a swig-a one-a them beers."

"I'ma pretend you di'n't say that shit."

"Nigga, you need a new thing, new flame," urged Blue Shoes.

"Tha's some Chris Brown shit. Song's old."

They went back and forth for a bit. Eventually Blue Shoes explained his theory of the benefits to having simultaneous East Bank and West Bank women in the stable. Stink elbowed him.

"Lookit. Ain't that bouncer work at the club with Kattrell? His shit got *fucked up*. Sure di'n't get none-a that stolen paper," Stink said.

Hutch overheard the stage whisper as he lurched and wheezed his way along the sidewalk. He glared at the source of the comment. "Got half a mind to stomp that Kid 'n' Play punk, but I'm on a mission. They knew me, though. That's no good."

A shop door to his right opened, three young women exited, and everyone on the sidewalk paused, rubber-necked, or were otherwise briefly frozen. The texting addicts looked away from their phones with only minor withdrawal symptoms. Even Hutch had a temporary break from soreness, coughing, and existential dread.

"Whoo-ee! She impossible," Stink said, punctuating the pause, and the buzz of life continued on.

"Get it, girl," called out a passer-by.

Two of the three women were regular neighborhood girls. They would likely go on to live perfectly fine regular lives.

Then there was Lyric.

She wore a short tight grey and white horizontally-striped dress, black lace-up sandals, large faux gold earrings, and black sunglasses. She had a number of tattoos on her arms and thighs.

Lyric's weave was attached to the crown of her head, pulled up from the sides, and collected in the middle front by a large black bow. On both sides of her head, instead of hair being entirely shaved off, she had leopard skin patterns. Scalp was the negative space.

She wore it all very well. Stink was at her mercy, and she knew it. Lyric was the kind of woman to make Lazarus raise himself from the grave.

"I might could go for some McDonald's," she floated.

Stink and Blue Shoes fell over each other trying to get to her.

After his instant of joyful paralysis, Hutch decided he needed a disguise. "If these triflin' punks can make me right off, Mr. C's people will too," he thought.

He looked ahead and saw a speck of Miss Melba's white outfit in the next block.

"I gotta do this quick."

Hutch ducked in a tourist shop and grabbed a few items by the front counter.

"Here. These. Hurry," he stressed.

While the clerk scanned them, rung them up, and handed

them back, Hutch took off his sweaty shirt and tossed it to the floor. He replaced it with a bright green t-shirt, tossed the strands of Mardi Gras beads over his neck, and placed a Mardi Gras-colored visor on his head.

"Don't have no pants or belt here?" he asked.

The clerk could've had an extensive wardrobe for sale and still would've emphatically shaken his head to the contrary.

"Alright." Hutch left the store and immediately looked to his right to check Miss Melba's progress before he tried to pick up the pace.

"I look like a damn clown, but man's gotta do what man's gotta do," he said. "Time to get what's mine."

A shirtless shoeless smiling man walked past Hutch, proclaiming the same thing he proclaimed all day long, "Don't you dare try to take over the world the same time as me." Hutch crinkled his face while he continued on.

The air on Canal was getting gustier the closer Hutch got to the river. He held one hand on his visor to keep it from flying off his head and used the other hand to keep his pants up as he hustled toward Miss Melba as fast as he could limp.

Once he got to Camp, the American street name on the other side of Canal from the European street name Chartres, he could hear the street preacher's patter from a megaphone amplified by the wind. The bearded zealot with his umbrella hat was set up between Chartres and Decatur.

Hutch was only half a block away from Miss Melba, but with his limp he wasn't making up any more ground than that.

"Where she goin'?" he wondered.

After another block, he had a suspicion, but when he saw her cross South Peters and make a slight right, he knew.

"No. No, no," he coughed.

Hutch was so fixated on Miss Melba that any street smarts he otherwise had were non-existent. He failed to see the man dodging traffic to cross Canal, heading right for him.

By the time Hutch got to South Peters, he saw the woman in white carrying the beer box slowly and steadily up the steps and entering Harrah's Casino.

"Gonna gamble away my fuckin' money," he said.

He was about to cross the street, when an out of breath man came running up to him.

"Excuse me, sir. Are you Raymond Pate? Hutch?"

Hutch panicked for a second but relaxed once he looked squarely at the speaker who was clearly not one of Mr. C's men. He coughed a few times before answering.

"Me? No, I'm, uh, Sam Gibbs. In town from Atlanta."

The man persisted. "Okay, but here's the thing. My name's Bobby Delery. I'm helping NOPD on a case. Just interviewed a guy named Cavallari at a club on Bourbon Street."

At that, Hutch's eyes triggered recognition. Delery caught it and continued.

"Cavallari gave me a description of an employee. You fit the description. You're dressed exactly like him. Limping like him. Have a bad smoker's cough. Look physically like him. I doubted the description, frankly, but then I saw and heard you across Canal."

Hutch brushed Delery off and crossed the street. It was obvious the man wasn't NOPD and didn't have any real power. But what did he mean about Mr. C describing the clown outfit? "He'd-a had my ass on the ground before asking a question if he was NOPD," Hutch thought. "Gotta get to Harrah's."

Delery walked with him. "I could call Commander Jones right now, but something's off. I think this is Raymond Pate, but he obviously doesn't have the money on him," he thought.

"Sir, sir…," Delery said.

Hutch scowled at him. "Let a man be. Can't a tourist see the sights and do a little gamblin'? Whatchu think I did?"

Delery was stuck. "Uh, Cavallari's place, Club Big Easy, uh, something's gone missing," he said sheepishly.

Hutch as an indignant Sam Gibbs shook his head and twisted his mouth as he limped along.

"Mmm hmm, that's how it is? See a black man, see a thief. We all look the same, all guilty to you crackers. Get outta my face."

"C'mon, that's not the way it is at all. In fact, I, uh, anyway, there are a lot of men out here, but I came to you for a reason. You're not Raymond Pate?"

Hutch laid it on thick. "I told you. Sam Gibbs from Atlanta. Let me be. Slowed me down enough already. Placate me, man."

They were almost at the steps leading up to Harrah's front door.

"I'll let him go in and then call Commander Jones. Maybe he's meeting an accomplice," Delery thought.

"Okay, okay. I'm just doing my job," he said. He stopped and looked up at the flags flapping in the breeze to the left of the casino. Hutch was now intent on making his way up the steps.

They both had their focus broken by an ageless man in drag screaming at a group of women wearing business suits. "Y'all a bunch of low down whores, skeezers, loose women," he ranted.

"Damn," said Hutch as he climbed.

"Reminds me of a lyric – "Preposterous like an androgynous misogynist,'" thought Delery. "Was that by Talib or Mos?"

The screaming brought a few bored glances from across Canal, where traffic was still backed up.

All of them turned away, except for the back seat passenger of an SUV in the right lane. The vehicle had pulled out of the Canal Place parking garage and was on its way back to the area near the Robertson overpass.

"Guys, hey. Look over on your left. Quick. That's Hutch. He's still in town," Johnny said.

"Johnny, you are desperate. That tourist cleaned out the safe? I do not think so," Pavel said.

"Pavel, I swear to you. I'd know him anywhere. Dunno why he's dressed like a fucking Mardi Gras float, but it's definitely him."

Kostya, the front seat passenger, scratched his ear. "If you are wasting our time, Mr. Yevchev will make you pay." In Russian he said, "Pavel, get over in the left lane and cross the street. You wait with the car. I will go in with shithead Johnny."

While they were stuck in traffic, Delery hunted through his pockets and shoulder bag. He finally found his phone, but it was broken.

"How the hell?" he wondered.

It took a few moments to realize that when the cops had him on the ground at Clouet, they must've broken it. "Fucking assholes," he fumed and started up the stairs.

Back when Bobby Delery unsuccessfully confronted Hutch in the guise of Sam Gibbs, Miss Melba Barnes accurately revealed for the first time that the large Abita Amber beer case contained money. She was not so forthcoming about its source.

The Harrah's greeter inside the second set of doors looked at Miss Melba quizzically as she came walking up with an irregular item.

"Ma'am, I need to see what's inside the box."

"Oh, mercy, of course," Miss Melba said, flipping the lid open. "The Lord told me this morning in church that I better bring my dead husband's pension here and increase it tenfold. Today's my lucky day." Her prayers had made her feel alright that a few of these light lies were necessary and harmed no one.

The greeter was a freckled man who didn't miss any tanning booth appointments. "Who knows?" he thought. "If she wants to bring in all that cash, who am I to say anything, considering." He'd seen money come in many ways, so this didn't surprise him much.

Miss Melba left the top of the beer box open, took a few more steps, and entered the bleeping, blipping, chiming world of slot machines to her right.

"I must act quickly," she said.

While Hutch and Delery did their dance outside, Miss Melba was involved in a flurry of activity. She'd planned it out in advance, and the first part went as expected. The security team watching the eye-in-the-sky cameras were curious, considered it unorthodox, but ultimately to the casino's benefit, so they let it go.

She next found her way back to a walkway and followed it around to her right, through the craps and roulette tables, past the cashiers who had a growing line of people, right by the entertainment area in the middle, and finally to a short line. Four people separated her from an occasional secret treat she'd indulged in back when she worked at the Marriott a few blocks away.

"I hope it's as good as it used to be," she murmured to the closest lady in front of her in line.

Her counterpart in age, dress, and appetite said, "It always is, my baby."

Eventually Miss Melba paid the cashier, was led to a table by the hostess, and had a waiter ask for her drink order. She smiled. "Sail On" by the Commodores was playing. A vast aroma was pervasive. All were happy and satisfied.

Miss Melba was at Harrah's lunch buffet.

"Sunday lunch costs twice as much as on weekdays," she chided. "But I guess it's alright. I'd like a cup of coffee and water, please." She placed the box under the table and made her way to collect her first plate.

She had a system for the buffet. Left to right. Miss Melba looked like a finch but ate like a buzzard.

For the first time since she left the house, she wasn't in direct possession of the beer case.

14

While Miss Melba was calmly working through a plate of fried catfish, mac & cheese, and mashed potatoes & gravy, it was all beginning to play out around the casino.

Hutch was searching for her. Delery was searching for Hutch. Kostya and Johnny were entering Harrah's to search for Hutch.

It may not be true to say that everything that rises must converge, but without question, if it does, it happens at the foot of Canal Street. Not just on land. Steps away, the river is full of pharmaceuticals, agricultural run-off, and other toxic slurries. If it's used or flushed by the rest of the country, down the river it goes.

Hutch expected Miss Melba to be playing high-stakes tables, so he bypassed the slot machines. "Maybe poker," he thought, but all he saw were a couple people per table, none of them an older black woman in all white.

Delery had never been in a casino before, so he began canvassing every inch of the place, slot machines included.

"I don't know if I'm struck more by the spirals of light overhead or how happy all the elderly people are playing the slots," he thought. Several of them had multiple buckets of chips gathered around their preferred computerized machine.

Kostya didn't trust Johnny, so they stayed together, but he'd given Johnny his gun back before they went inside.

"You better be right," Kostya said menacingly to Johnny.

"I'm telling you. I'd know him anywhere."

They saw numerous tourists with some semblance of Mardi Gras colors, but none were Hutch.

Harrah's security was discreet, mostly a few men in yellow

shirts. Everyone knew, though, with so much money at stake throughout the casino, it wouldn't take much for an overt elevated presence to make itself known.

Kostya figured that if Johnny was right, the preferable way of securing Hutch was near one of the entrance doors around the casino, so they could quickly get him outside. The streets were their turf. Pavel was waiting on Canal in the car.

The Russian and Sicilian stalked past the cashiers who exchanged casino chips for cash, credit card, or line of credit. Vice versa, as well. They were the bank.

Meanwhile, Hutch was perplexed. He was coming up short and getting more confused, worried, and angry by the minute. Restrooms were now a possibility.

"Why not? Here somewhere, gamblin' away my money. Wasn't in the high-roller room," he said.

In the meantime, Miss Melba was working on her second plate. Turkey & gravy, barbecue brisket, and greens.

Hutch limped through the slot areas in case she was walking around, which brought him back to a Starbucks near the Canal entrance. His nerves were frayed.

"Small coffee," he said to the barista.

As trained, the earnest teenager responded, "A Tall? Would you like to make that a Venti for just a little more?"

Hutch stared her down. "Just gimme the damn coffee."

After he paid and collected his drink, he turned to leave, but she was relentless.

"Sir, here's your receipt. If you go to this website," she said, circling it with a pen, "and fill out the customer satisfaction survey, you'll get a discount next time. I'd appreciate it if you say we exceeded your expectations."

Hutch gave her a look that said, "Are you kidding me?" Though he didn't reply, someone else did.

"There are no surveys where he is going," said a voice with

Russian-accented English.

Johnny knocked the coffee out of Hutch's hand before it could get thrown at either of them.

"Have a nice motherfucking day," Kostya said with a grim smile to the horrified barista.

Hutch tried to call out for help, but all that rose from his throat was a raw bout of coughing. Kostya and Johnny roughly led him to the door with guns stuck into his side. The casino greeter called security.

When a few yellow shirts ran past Delery seconds later, he followed them, hoping their urgency was connected to the man he'd been trying to find. By the time security and Delery made it out the front door, Kostya and Johnny had Hutch down the steps and midway to a waiting SUV. Something else froze Delery and the security guards in place.

A red streetcar was on its way up Canal. Another was heading the other direction. From their view, elevated by ten steps up, Delery and a half dozen Harrah's security guards saw a couple men racing across the street directly toward the two and their captive. The streetcars blocked the view by the threesome.

Minutes before, Stink, Lyric, and Lyric's two sidekicks left McDonald's and walked with Blue Shoes to the ferry terminal where Canal ended. Blue Shoes was on his way to see his Algiers honey, and the others were passing the time.

Blue Shoes had his head down, texting her, when Stink said, "Look, Blue. Them whities got that bouncer!"

"Aw, fuck no. I ain't sleepin' on that. Them bleach-ass muthafuckas ain't takin' that nigga," Blue Shoes said. He pulled out his .45 and started across Canal.

Stink followed him with a drawn .38. They both ran right through the midst of backed-up cars in the three lanes on their side of Canal.

Lyric looked on with adoring eyes, holding their McDonald's

bags.

"That's my boo. He even shoot white mens. Fi'in' to get two right quick," she bragged to the others. "Ooh, watch this."

At that point, the two streetcars shielded surface level eyes on both sides of the street, but seconds later the scene opened up again.

Kostya and Johnny were pushing a limping Hutch off to the right where the SUV was idling. Pavel was waiting inside it, behind the wheel.

Blue Shoes and Stink were now across Canal, racing behind the three just ahead.

And the seven, Delery included, right outside the casino doors saw it all play out.

Four men had guns. All were right-handed.

Kostya who was on the left of Hutch, was the first to turn at the sound of quick footsteps. Hutch was next, followed by Johnny.

Hutch was big enough that Johnny, who was on his right, couldn't make a simple turn to his left to shoot. He had to spin and take a couple steps away from Hutch before firing. Johnny caught three bullets from Blue Shoes, one of them to the heart.

Kostya missed Stink, and Stink missed Kostya, but as momentum carried them closer together, Kostya put down Stink with a Russian-made pistol. Lyric's screams could be heard across the river.

Blue Shoes had been an erratic shot up until a month before, but he saw his practicing with bottles and cans in a City Park field pay off when he riddled Kostya's body with bullets.

Hutch had been terrified to move, what with all the bullets flying. He looked at the fallen men to his sides and at Blue Shoes, hoping the shooting was done.

"Little brother, y'all had me wonderin'. This is…," Hutch said. A short blip sound preceded Hutch's keeling over. He bent at the waist before collapsing.

Pavel was a far better shooter than Kostya. He intended his second shot for the other man standing, but Blue Shoes took off running, and the Russian knew time as short. There was rarely NOPD presence on Canal Street, but they'd eventually show up.

Pavel unscrewed his silencer, put the safety on his .45, and tucked them both away in the vehicle. He reversed the SUV back to Kostya's bloody body, opened the back door on the right, and pulled his fellow Russian up into the back seat. Pavel took a right at the end of Canal and raced off.

Blue Shoes put his gun away while he ran with Lyric and friends back to the stolen Corolla he'd driven downtown.

"Holy shit," Delery said.

The Harrah's security guards saw him for the first time.

"One of you call NOPD," Delery said. "I'm working with them, but my phone's broken."

He went down to the carnage.

Stink moved and said, "Help me." Delery assured him that the EMS would be there soon. In squatting down, Delery came to a realization.

"You were one of the guys who tried to rob me earlier," he said. Stink was as helpless as an infant, so Delery kept his "Fuck you" to himself and turned around in disgust. No one else seemed alive.

Delery checked the pockets of the dead black man. Both driver's license and passport were in the name of Maurice Richard of Texas. The man had money on him, but nowhere near the amount that was stolen. "Not Raymond Pate, but not Sam Gibbs from Atlanta either," mused Delery. "Or they're aliases."

Delery waited there until all the first responders arrived, then he and the security guards told them what'd happened.

"I need to go inside. Wash up. Use the bathroom," Delery said. "I'll be back shortly. Have someone call Commander Jones then," he thought.

When he'd initially been looking for the man who may have been Hutch and made his way through the casino, back to where he remembered seeing the restrooms, Delery hadn't paid attention to the dining room.

This time, when he passed it and looked to his right, a sight caught his eye. The woman he'd seen earlier walking across the Claiborne overpass, right in the heart of where Clint Olson was killed and where the glowing man had been. Now she was here, sitting and eating. And a beer case at her feet. Cavallari had mentioned a beer case. Delery got in line for the buffet, still carrying his bag of books.

He was pleasantly surprised that the piped-in music, 70's soul, was better than most of what he'd heard on Bourbon Street.

After making his way through the payment line, more of his casino buffet preconceptions were shattered. The tables were filled with a racially mixed group, and only a few of them were obese. The vast majority were over sixty, though.

Delery asked the hostess if he could be seated at a particular table. It faced the lady dressed in white who had a beer case below her table. He wasn't going to let her out of his sight.

She got up after emptying her plate, so he rose too, not waiting to place his drink order. Left his notebook and pen on the table to show it was taken. He found it odd that she left the beer case unprotected. It was all he could do not to go over to it.

Delery followed her to the approximate middle of the hot food area. He saw her place a vegetarian egg roll, couple pieces of crab Rangoon, serving spoon of beef & broccoli, and half a serving spoon of shrimp fried rice on her plate. He quickly filled up his own plate in a similar way and walked at a healthy pace back to his table.

Though she was paying little mind to anything but lunch, he tried not to let his studying glances seem too obvious. He hadn't heard her speak to anyone, so he only had a physical description.

"Mid-60's or older. Dressed all in white, so she was at church before coming here. By herself, so her husband's probably passed away and she has few friends. Short curly white hair. Glasses. Petite. Eats like she walks, not in a rush, so she's not in a hurry. And that Abita case under the table. What I wouldn't give to open it," he thought.

Delery didn't know how to better initiate contact, so, leaving his plate of Asian food half-eaten, he got up and walked over to her table.

"Excuse me, ma'am, but I believe I saw you earlier. The Claiborne overpass back by Franklin," he said.

Miss Melba looked up.

"Yes, that was me, young man. On my way to church. It's Sunday."

Delery didn't like the dynamics of his standing over her.

"Ma'am, my name's Bobby Delery. Would you mind if I sit down?"

"Don't you have a table? I'm fine with my own company."

Delery saw no other choice but to be forward, so he sat down across from her.

"Can't a woman have some peace?" she sputtered.

"I apologize, but please. I need to ask you a few questions."

"Young man, what would you possibly have to ask me?"

"You carried that big beer case a long way," he questioned in the form of a statement.

Miss Melba put down her fork and lifted the box. Leaning toward him, she opened up the pieces of lid. Empty. Delery was stunned.

"Who couldn't carry an empty box?" she scoffed.

"No disrespect, but it looked like it was really heavy when I saw you with it."

Anger flashed in her eyes. "If you must know, I had some canned food to donate. I kept the box for gambling after lunch, though. Maybe I'll win. What do you care about an old woman and a box anyway?"

Other diners at the tables and booths around them were starting to stir and whisper about the interaction.

He laid it on the line. "I'll tell you why I'm asking. What's your name, by the way?"

"If you must know, it's Melba Barnes."

"Mrs. Barnes, I'm asking you all this because of my job. I'm a criminologist. NOPD asked me to assist them with a case. A club over on Bourbon Street had a lot of money go missing. People are after this money. Men may have just been killed for it. Right outside."

She shuddered. "Killed? All the money's from Bourbon Street?" She stopped, realizing she'd said too much.

"Yes, ma'am. A man was taken by gunpoint out of Harrah's. He and the two men who had him were all shot and killed. A young guy was shot too, but it looks like he'll be okay."

Miss Melba was curious and couldn't resist saying, "I saw an odd man earlier. He had a limp. Coughed a lot. Big too."

Delery wondered if she was implicating herself. This sounded like the same person he'd questioned. "Was he dressed like a tourist? Mardi Gras clothes and beads?"

"Oh, no. Not at all," she said, confusing Delery once again.

He tried one last ditch effort. "Do you know that man's name, Mrs. Barnes?" he asked.

"How would I know that?"

"Let me ask you this way. Do the names Raymond Pate, Hutch, Sam Gibbs, or Maurice Richard mean anything to you?"

She was ready to extricate herself from the questioning.

"Of course not. Why would they?" she snapped. "My food's getting cold. Do you mind letting me be? It's been less than a pleasure."

Delery realized he'd pushed hard enough for the time being. His instincts were telling him she was connected in some way. New Orleans was a small interconnected city of fewer than 400,000 people, but when circumstantial aspects start piling up, there's probably a reason.

He excused himself and started to rise from the chair at the same time a tall jowly old white man wearing a strikingly large fishing hat and particularly short nylon shorts came jingling up to the table, all knees and exuberance. His age spots were the color of subdivisions everywhere.

Before Miss Melba could say a word, the man held up his bucket and blurted out to her, "I decided tuh come over here to yuh, since I had this coupon for a free buffet. I know you told us all you'd come to us, but hey, my belly was callin'. Didn't win anything much, but it was great fun. Thanks for all the chips. I've got yours, just like you asked. Twenty-five of 'em. Thousand dollar ones. Want to count 'em to make sure?"

Both Miss Melba and Delery were at a loss for words, she from frustration and he from confusion. He knew, though, that the confusion was leading somewhere useful.

She managed an awkward "Thank you" and painstakingly dumped the casino chips from the gambler's bucket into her beer case.

"Again, I much 'ppreciate it. Gettin' a bite tuh eat 'fore headin' back to Texarkana," he said and loped off.

Delery sat back down.

"Mrs. Barnes, I think you know more than you've let on. A stranger brought you $25,000 like it was nothing," he said.

She knew it was coming but half-heartedly tried to brush it off. "I don't know what you mean."

Delery bluffed. He held up his broken phone and got bold.

"If I press redial, I can get an NOPD commander on the phone. Not to mention all the cops outside. I'm not a cop, though. Just trying to figure things out. The money that's missing…there are some bad people looking for it. They're probably responsible for the bodies outside. If you have some of it, your life's in danger."

Her eyes searched his. She saw someone who meant well but she couldn't totally trust. He saw the first sign of her vulnerability and fear. Also a sense of déjà vu that took him back to his childhood.

"Are you really so concerned about my safety, or do you just want to keep the status quo? If money's gone missing from bad people like you say, what'll it get used for if they get it back? Or if they police find it first?"

"I understand where you're coming from, but the fact remains that you're potentially at risk," Delery emphasized, "depending on where the $25,000 for those chips came from. Look, there are cops and probably mobsters looking for the money. I think some of the cops are looking on behalf of the mobsters. It's better you deal with me."

She sighed. "I understand what you're saying, but who are you? All I see is a man who tells me he's with the police, but he's not actual police. Who are you? Why should I trust you, especially since you're a…"

Delery took a long pause. "Mrs. Barnes, this is awkward. I'm sure you've dealt with a lot of prejudice over the years. Are you uncomfortable, at least in part, because you see a white man trying to get one over on a black woman?"

"You're the one who said it. I've worked with whites over the years. But… if I feel uneasy, that's my right. You don't know what I've been through."

Delery looked at her solidly and took a deep breath.

"This isn't something I usually talk about," he said. "I've learned it's better not to bring it up."

Miss Melba looked at him, wondering.

"Ma'am, I'm black," he said.

15

Miss Melba pursed her lips and folded her arms. She remembered the whitest white man she had ever seen, face down in her yard. This was different, though. She raised her voice.

"Don't tell me you're one of those white men who likes black music and black women, so you think you're black. Let me tell *you* something. The low down Klan used to book black bands for their functions. As for women, we all know what color master liked back in the slave days," she said.

The surrounding diners looked at each other cross-eyed, their faces stretching every which way as they heard the neighboring conversation getting real.

"I'm black, Mrs. Barnes," he said again.

"Maybe you've seen that Chappelle Show and think you know about black folks? Think we do nothing but sit around and talk about Rick James."

Delery closed his eyes. Being back home had him feeling emotional.

"I know I don't look it," he said. "A reverse oreo, that's me. My dad was white. Mama's black. She and both my brothers black as anyone in this room."

He paused before continuing on.

"I grew up in the 70's. The decade when our people finally had our own options. In our house, it was Muhammed Ali, not Bruce Jenner. Soul Train, not American Bandstand. James Baldwin, not Norman Mailer. Pam Grier, not Farrah Fawcett. I never saw Mama again after my parents split up, but right now your eyes remind me of hers."

Miss Melba was still skeptical, rightly so.

"Your answers don't answer. How do I know this isn't an elaborate story you prepared?"

He shrugged. "I don't know, ma'am. I can only say it's something I don't bring up much if I don't have to. It makes white people suspicious. Black people think I'm an ofay trying to front. Generally speaking. I realize things have been easier for me, all in all."

She nodded and thought, was about to speak, but corrected herself.

"Give me a minute. While I'm thinking, would you do something for me? I like to finish my meal with a lemon square. They're right over there in the desserts," she pointed. "Don't worry. I'm not going anywhere."

Delery initially kept looking back while on his way to the menagerie of desserts but realized she was staying put. He got a lemon square for each of them.

When he returned, she smiled warmly, but her eyes still pierced.

"I have three questions for you. Answer them right, and I'll believe you. Alright?"

He silently affirmed but furrowed his face, not knowing what was in store for him.

"While you answer, I'm going to start in on my lemon square. First one. BPT. What is it?"

Delery leaned back. This one was easy.

"BPT is Black People Time, the idea that we're always late. You don't hear CPT used much anymore. Of course, in New Orleans, it should just be NOPT. Almost everybody's running behind here, regardless of race," he said.

"Alright." She nodded in his favor. "Number two. Your mama's black? Tell me how she did her hair."

"Sure." He leaned in. "Like I said, I grew up in the 70's, so she kept her hair natural. But when she got a part-time job, she

—159—

had to straighten. Mama used a hot comb, the kind you put on the stove to heat it up. I remember the smell of the previous oils and greases."

"She ever burn herself?" Miss Melba asked.

"Knicked her ear once. Only time I heard her curse. After I was nine, I don't know what she did. I went away with my dad."

"The things we do with our hair. That'll make anybody talk salty," she mused. "Alright. Last one. In church, what happens after the preacher's altar call?"

"I haven't been to church in a while," he said, wondering if it was a trick question, "but after the altar call and maybe prayer, the pastor calls on the congregation to come forward and give what they can. Some people tithe, but others wait until after the sermon to see if the preacher moved us, made us feel blessed, put his all into it. The preacher might keep the congregation there for a while, trying to get them to give. It's not only that we're skeptical people, for good reason. We just don't give up our money until somebody can show us something. Assuming you're talking about a black church."

Delery looked at her expectantly and nervously ate a piece of his lemon square. She'd already finished hers.

Miss Melba bobbed her head several times before she spoke.

"Well, I'll be. Goodness, that beats the devil with a shovel. I thought it was a set up at first, you coming up to me. You are the whitest looking black man I've ever seen. Not albino either."

She laughed and lowered her voice.

"Alright, Bobby. It's time to tell what I've been up to. I'm only telling you this because I need some help to finish today's journey. You can talk the talk. Now it's time to walk the walk. You said there are a lot of police and criminals and criminal police looking for the money?"

"Yes, ma'am. Look how much cash we're talking. Wait, do

you know how much it is?"

"Yes, but I didn't know where it came from until you said. It got unintentionally brought to me by a person who obviously didn't own it. Whitest looking white man I've ever seen."

Delery's eyes lit up. It had to be the guy he'd seen earlier who'd gotten away.

"I knew, though, that much money in a beer box had to be dirty. Am I wrong?"

Delery agreed.

"What do you do with dirty money?" she asked.

"You clean it," he answered.

"What do you do?" she repeated.

"Clean it," he said.

"Yes, you do," she said. "That's what I've been up to. With some help. By the way, your mama really let you watch those Pam Grier movies?"

He smiled. "Of course not, but we'd trade pictures in school."

"I bet you did. I wasn't born yesterday. Before I got here, a big limping man had been following me all the way back from Franklin. Maybe one of the men who got killed," she said. "Another one was after me too, but he stopped following for some reason."

Miss Melba put her hand out.

"Let's back up. Listen to me now. When I found the money, there were ninety-seven packets. Each packet had 100 marked $100 bills. New crisp ones. $10,000 per packet. I tossed two packets into the wind back by the bus stop at Canal and Rampart for a distraction. That gave me a head start from the ones after me. I only got rid of that much money because I couldn't keep putting them off from getting the box. I tithed one packet at church too. Didn't need to wait until after the sermon. Kept one packet in my purse, just in case."

She grinned about referencing Delery's answer to her earlier question.

"That left me with $930,000. I've never gambled a day in my life, but I am fond of the buffet. From being here, eating in the casino, I know a little how things operate. So, I took a chance on self-interest and trust."

She took a sip of water.

"What choice did I have? The minute I got inside Harrah's, I gathered thirty-one people playing the slots. Most around my age. Each of them got three packets of money. That's $30,000 a piece, Bobby."

"You gave away over $900,000 to slot machine gamblers?" Delery asked, incredulous.

She shrugged. "Like I said, there wasn't much choice. A desperate man was after the beer box. All that dirty money to clean. Yes, I hoped for honest gamblers. Still hoping."

Miss Melba checked her watch.

"I've only got a couple minutes, then it'll be an hour, so I'll talk quick. Again, the thirty-one people each got $30,000. They were told to convert $25,000 of that into $1,000 chips with the cashier for me. I let them skim off $5,000 for their own chips. They were to gamble away and wait for me to come collect my chips an hour later. As you know, one of the thirty-one couldn't follow directions."

She gestured with her thumb off toward fishing hat man on the other side of the dining room.

"I wanted them to wait an hour so that anyone after me would see my empty beer box and just go away."

Delery nodded knowingly.

"So, yes, I gave them a total of $155,000 to help me out, but I'm about to go over to the slot machines and collect $775,000 in $1,000 chips."

"Ma'am, I'm not totally following," he said. "You're still going to have all that money in casino chips."

"That's the second part, Bobby. First convert the marked dirty money to chips so the $100's couldn't be traced. Next, those chips are going to organizations who need the money. They'll send someone in here with the chips to convert them back to cash. I'll need your help getting out of here safely with all the chips. Delivering them too. Be thinking about that. Let's go load this up."

She picked up the box and stood. Delery waited.

"Mrs. Barnes, one question. What line of work were you in before you retired?"

"I was an accountant for the Marriott Hotel, baby. What'd you think?"

They left the dining room and walked around to the area of slot machines near the Canal Street entrance. Friendly faces met Miss Melba, and she had thirty buckets of $1,000 chips poured into the beer case.

After goodbye's were said, Delery whispered to Miss Melba, "We can't go back out on Canal. I saw there's a way to get over to the hotel."

They walked through the connecting underground tunnel, Miss Melba insisting on carrying the box. They came out at the hotel shortly after.

"Why don't you wait in the lobby. I'm going to my car and driving back here. While you're waiting, will you get the addresses for the organizations you want these chips to go to? The concierge will have a phone book. Find out where the closest UPS store is too," he requested. "I'd let you use my phone, but it's broken."

She gave him a look and nodded knowingly.

Delery went outside and briskly walked Poydras a few blocks before turning toward Canal Street. He wound through the Quarter, retrieved his car, and took Rampart over to Poydras.

After picking up Miss Melba, they went to the UPS store

on St. Charles, and Delery darted inside. When he returned, he had ten shoebox-sized shipping boxes, as she'd requested, along with packing tape, a marker, and a ream of paper.

There in the car, he folded the boxes up, and taped them in place. She carefully counted out the chips and distributed them to each box.

Five boxes got seventy-seven $1,000 chips. Five boxes got seventy-eight chips. Using her left hand, Miss Melba used the marker to write, "Private Donation – Take to Harrah's to redeem," on ten pieces of paper. She was right-handed, writing as a lefty for anonymity. After a note was placed inside each box, Delery sealed them all with tape. Miss Melba wrote the name of the organization on the box.

Next they made the rounds. At each address, Delery ran up with the corresponding box and left it on a step, behind bushes, or wherever it could be slightly tucked away. He rang no doorbells.

After a couple hours, their work was done. Delery drove Miss Melba home. Along the way they passed a swarm of hopeful types, some flea-bitten, others fresh-faced. All had heard through the grapevine about the missing money and were traipsing around like gold prospectors.

"Bobby, thank you," she said. "This was the right thing to do."

They embraced.

"I think you're right, ma'am," he said.

"You can call me Melba," she said. "I'd invite you in so you could see Allen Toussaint acting his charming self, but after all the activity today, I need to rest."

Delery was ready to believe anything at that point.

"Wait, Allen Toussaint is here?" he asked, pointing at the house. "*The* Allen Toussaint?"

"Of course. Moses too."

She squeezed his arm.

"But they're cats."

"Oh, I see. Melba, can I ask you one last question?"

"Of course, Bobby."

"What are you going to do with the last $10,000 you said you'd kept just in case? Those bills are marked."

She said, "I guess I don't know quite yet, but the money needs to go to Harrah's and get swapped out in a few days." She paused and smiled. "What I do know is to get this thing done, I had to keep skimming off the top for everyone."

With that, she left the car.

Delery drove until he found a working payphone. He'd written Commander Jones' phone number in his notebook, which he'd tucked into the glove box when he'd retrieved the car to pick up Miss Melba.

He opened the glove box and pulled out the notebook. It was stuffed with something. He opened it and counted fifty $100 bills. Each had the telltale small highlighter dot in the top left corner. Miss Melba must've stashed them there when he was inside the UPS store buying supplies. He knew what to do with the money.

Delery let loose a big grin. He was sweaty, wrinkled, and tired, but he didn't care.

"Welcome to New Orleans," he said, looking around. He folded the money and shoved it into his pocket.

That same evening in two instances, and the next morning for all the others, those from nine New Orleans organizations involved in the arts, tutoring, adult education, or job training were delighted to discover their mysterious boxes of casino chips. The SPCA too.

Others in the city weren't so happy. They didn't have quiet engines for days to come. Their plagued minds stayed on the boil. The mean streets became a little meaner.

Delery found Jones' number and left a voice mail message explaining the bloodbath he'd seen after following the trail down Canal Street. He also said that he was at a brick wall to proceed further with the case.

"And Commander Jones, I won't need any officers to assist after all with my refrigerator delivery. I'm going to take it easy the rest of the day. I'll definitely call in that favor at some point, though."

Delery flipped a few more pages to see the name Ellis Smith and her email address again. He savored the recent memory and hoped for what it might lead to. She was radiant. He couldn't wait to see her again.

After reflecting for a couple minutes, he walked with a light step to the car, and drove off, ready to start unpacking.

Michael Allen Zell is a New Orleans-based novelist, essayist, and playwright. Zell's work has been published in *The Los Angeles Review of Books, Cerise Press, Disonare, Entrepot, Exquisite Corpse, NOLA Defender, Room 220*, and *Sleepingfish*. *Errata*, his first novel, was named a 'Top 10 Book of 2012' by *The Times-Picayune*. His first play, *What Do You Say To A Shadow?*, was named a 'Top 10 Play of the Year' in 2013 by *The Times-Picayune*. He has worked as a bookseller since 2001.

Lavender Ink
New Orleans
lavenderink.org

CPSIA information can be obtained at www.ICGtesting.com
Printed in the USA
LVOW11s2318041015

456898LV00004B/165/P